DARK MATTER

DARK MATTER

MICHELLE PAVER

ISIS
LARGE PRINT
Oxford

First published in Great Britain 2010
by
Orion Books
An imprint of The Orion Publishing Group Ltd.

Published in Large Print 2011 by ISIS Publishing Ltd.,
7 Centremead, Osney Mead, Oxford OX2 0ES
by arrangement with
The Orion Publishing Group Ltd.
An Hachette UK Company

British Library Cataloguing in Publication Data
Paver, Michelle.
   Dark matter.
   1. Artic regions - - Discovery and exploration - -
   British - - Fiction.
   2. Ghost stories.
   3. Large type books.
   I. Title
   823.9'2–dc22

ISBN 978–0–7531–8808–8 (hb)
ISBN 978–0–7531–8809–5 (pb)

Printed and bound in Great Britain by
T. J. International Ltd., Padstow, Cornwall

Embleton Grange
Cumberland

24th November 1947

Dear Dr Murchison,

Forgive me for this rather belated reply to your letter.

You will I am sure understand why I found it hard to entertain your enquiry with any pleasure. To be blunt, you evoked painful memories which I have tried for ten years to forget. The expedition crippled a friend of mine and killed another. It is not something I care to revisit.

You mentioned that you are working on a monograph on "phobic disorders", by which I take it you mean abnormal fears. I regret that I can tell you nothing which would be of assistance. Moreover, I fail to see how the "case" (as you put it) of Jack Miller could provide appropriate material for such a work.

In your letter, you conceded that you know little of Spitsbergen, or indeed of anywhere else in what is often called the High Arctic. This is to be expected. Few people do. Forgive me, though, if I question how you would then propose to understand what it can do to a man to overwinter there. To battle the loneliness and desolation;

yes, even with the many comforts that our modern age affords. Above all, to endure the endless dark. And as circumstances dictated, it was Jack's misfortune to be there alone.

I don't think we will ever learn the truth of what happened at Gruhuken. However I know enough to be convinced that something terrible took place. And whatever it was, Dr Murchison, it was real. It was not the result of some phobic disorder. And in this respect I would add that before entering politics I undertook some years of study in the sciences, and thus feel myself entitled on two counts to be considered a reasonable judge of evidence. Moreover, no one has ever doubted my sanity, or proposed to include my "case" in a monograph.

I don't know how you came by the knowledge that Jack Miller kept a journal on the expedition, but you are right, he did. I saw him writing in it many times. We used to rag him about it, and he took this in good part, although he never showed us its contents. No doubt the journal would, as you suggest, explain much of what happened; but it has not survived, and I cannot ask Jack himself.

Thus I fear that I am unable to help you. I wish you well with your work. However I must ask you not to apply to me again.

Yours sincerely,
Algernon Carlisle

CHAPTER
ONE

Jack Miller's journal
7th January 1937

It's all over, I'm not going.

I can't spend a year in the Arctic with that lot. They arrange to "meet for a drink", then give me a grilling, and make it pretty clear what they think of a grammar-school boy with a London degree. Tomorrow I'll write and tell them where to put their sodding expedition.

The way they watched me when I entered that pub.

It was off the Strand, so not my usual haunt, and full of well-to-do professional types. A smell of whisky and a fug of expensive cigar smoke. Even the barmaid was a cut above.

The four of them sat at a corner table, watching me shoulder my way through. They wore Oxford bags and tweed jackets with that elegantly worn look which you only acquire at country house weekends. Me in my scuffed shoes and my six-guinea Burton's suit. Then I saw the drinks on the table and thought, Christ, I'll have to buy a round, and I've only got a florin and a threepenny bit.

We said our hellos, and they relaxed a bit when they heard that I don't actually drop my aitches, but I was so busy wondering if I could afford the drinks that it took me a while to work out who was who.

Algie Carlisle is fat and freckled, with pale eyelashes and sandy-red hair; he's a follower rather than a leader, who relies on his pals to tell him what to think. Hugo Charteris-Black is thin and dark, with the face of an Inquisitor looking forward to putting a match to another heretic. Teddy Wintringham has bulging eyes that I think he thinks are penetrating. And Gus Balfour is a handsome blond hero straight out of *The Boy's Own Paper*. All in their mid-twenties, but keen to appear older: Carlisle and Charteris-Black with moustaches, Balfour and Wintringham with pipes clamped between their teeth.

I knew I hadn't a chance, so I thought to hell with it, give it to them straight: offer yourself like a lamb to the slaughter (if lambs can snarl). So I did. Bexhill Grammar, Open Scholarship to UCL. The slump putting paid to my dreams of being a physicist, followed by seven years as an export clerk at Marshall Gifford.

They took it in silence, but I could see them thinking, *Bexhill, how frightfully middle class; all those ghastly mock-Tudor dwellings by the sea. And University College . . . not exactly Oxbridge, is it?*

Gus Balfour asked about Marshall Gifford, and I said, "They make high-quality stationery, they export all over the world." I felt myself reddening. God Almighty, Jack, you sound like Mr Pooter.

Then Algie Carlisle, the plump one, asked if I shoot.

"Yes," I said crisply. (Well, I *can* shoot, thanks to old Mr Carwardine, DO, retired, of the Malaya Protectorate, who used to take me on to the Downs after rabbits; but that's not the kind of shooting this lot are used to.)

4

No doubt Carlisle was thinking the same thing, because he asked rather doubtfully if I'd got my own gun.

"Service pattern rifle," I said. "Nothing special, but it does OK."

That elicited a collective wince, as if they'd never heard slang before.

Teddy Wintringham mentioned wirelessing and asked if I knew my stuff. I said I should think so, after six years of night technical school, both the General and Advanced courses; I wanted something practical that would keep me in touch with physics. (More Mr Pooter. Stop *wittering*.)

Wintringham smiled thinly at my discomfort. "No idea what any of that means, old chap. But I'm told that we rather need someone like you."

I gave him a cheery smile and pictured blasting a hole in his chest with said rifle.

It can't have been that cheery, though, because Gus Balfour — the Honourable Augustus Balfour — sensed that things were veering off track, and started telling me about the expedition.

"There are two aims," he began, looking very earnest and more like a schoolboy hero than ever. "One, to study High Arctic biology, geology and ice dynamics. To that end we'll be establishing a base camp on the coast, and another on the icecap itself — which is why we'll be needing a team of dogs. Secondly, and more importantly, a meteorological survey, transmitting observations three times a day for a year, to the Government forecasting system. That's why we're getting help from the Admiralty and the War Office. They seem to think our data will be of use if — well, if there's another war."

There was an uneasy pause, and I could see them hoping we wouldn't get side-tracked into discussing the situation in Spain and the neutrality of the Low Countries.

Turning my back on world politics, I said, "And you're planning to achieve all that with only five men?"

This drew sharp glances from the others, but Gus Balfour took it in good part. "I know it's a tall order. But you see, we have thought about this. The plan is, Algie will be chief huntsman, dog-driver and geologist. Teddy's the photographer and medico. Hugo's the glaciologist for the icecap side of things. We'll all lend a hand with the meteorology. I'll be the biologist and, um, Expedition Leader. And you'll be —" He broke off with a rueful laugh. "Sorry, we *hope* you'll be our communications man."

He seemed genuinely keen to win me over, and I couldn't help feeling flattered. Then Hugo Charteris-Black, the Inquisitor, spoiled it by demanding to know why I wanted to come, and was I quite sure I understood what I'd be letting myself in for?

"You do realise what the winter will be like?" he said, fixing me with his coal-black stare. "Four months of darkness. Think you can take it?"

I gritted my teeth and told him that was why I wanted to go: for the challenge.

Oh, they liked that. I expect it's the sort of thing you're taught at public school. I was glad I hadn't told them the real reason. They'd have been mortified if I'd said I was desperate.

I couldn't put off buying my round any longer. Pints for Algie Carlisle, Teddy Wintringham and Hugo Charteris-Black (at sevenpence a go), a half for me (that's another threepence halfpenny). I was thinking I wasn't going to manage it when Gus Balfour said, "Nothing for me." He made quite a convincing job of it, but I could tell that he was trying to help me out. It made me feel ashamed.

After that, things went OK for a while. We worked our way through our drinks, and then Gus Balfour glanced at the others and nodded, and said to me, "Well, now, Miller. Would you care to join our expedition?"

I'm afraid I got a bit choked. "Um, yes," I said. "Yes, I should think I would."

The others looked merely relieved, but Gus Balfour seemed genuinely delighted. He kept clapping me on the back and saying, "Good show, good show!" I don't think he was putting it on.

After that we fixed our next meeting, and then I said my goodbyes and headed for the door. But at the last moment, I glanced over my shoulder — and caught Teddy Wintringham's grimace and Algie Carlisle's fatalistic shrug. *Not exactly a sahib, but I suppose he'll have to do.*

Stupid to be so angry. I wanted to march back and smash their smug faces into their overpriced drinks. Do you know what it's like to be poor? Hiding your cuffs, inking the holes in your socks? Knowing that you smell because you can't afford more than one bath a week? Do you think I like it?

I knew then it was hopeless. I couldn't be part of their expedition. If I can't put up with them for a couple of hours, how could I stand a whole year? I'd end up killing someone.

Later

....

Jack, what the hell are you doing? What the hell are you doing?

As I headed home, the fog on the Embankment was terrible. Buses and taxicabs creeping past, muffled cries of paper boys. Street lamps just murky yellow pools, illuminating nothing. God, I hate fog. The stink, the streaming eyes. The taste of it in your throat, like bile.

There was a crowd on the pavement, so I stopped. They were watching a body being pulled from the river. Someone said it must be another poor devil who couldn't find work.

Leaning over the parapet, I saw three men on a barge hauling a bundle of sodden clothes on to the deck. I made out a wet round head, and a forearm which one of the gaffs had ripped open. The flesh was ragged and grey, like torn rubber.

I wasn't horrified, I've seen a dead body before. I was curious. And as I stared at the black water I wondered how many others had died in it, and why doesn't it have more ghosts?

You'd have thought that brush with mortality would have put things in perspective, but it didn't. I was still seething when I reached the tube station. In fact I was so angry that I overshot my stop and had to get out at Morden and backtrack to Tooting.

The fog was thicker in Tooting. It always is. As I groped my way up my road, I felt like the last one left alive.

The stairs to the third floor smelt of boiled cabbage and Jeyes' Fluid. It was so cold I could see my breath.

My room wasn't any better, but I had my anger to keep me warm. I grabbed my journal and spewed it all out. To hell with them, I'm not going.

That was a while ago.

My room is freezing. The gas jet casts a watery glimmer that shudders whenever a tram thunders past. I've got no coal, two cigarettes, and twopence halfpenny to last till payday. I'm so hungry my stomach's given up rumbling because it knows there isn't any point.

I'm sitting on my bed with my overcoat on. It smells of fog. And of the journey I've taken twice a day, six days a week, for seven years with all the other grey people. And of Marshall Gifford, where they call me "College" because I've got a degree, and where for three pounds a week I track shipments of paper to places I'll never see.

I'm twenty-eight years old and I hate my life. I never have the time or the energy to work out how to change it. On Sundays I trail round a museum to keep warm, or lose myself in a library book, or fiddle with the wireless. But Monday's already looming. And always I've got this panicky feeling inside, because I know I'm getting nowhere, just keeping myself alive.

Tacked above the mantelpiece is a picture called "A Polar Scene" that I cut out from the *Illustrated London News*. A vast, snowy land and a black sea dotted with icebergs. A tent, a sledge and some husky dogs. Two men in Shackleton gear standing over the carcass of a polar bear.

That picture is nine years old. Nine years ago I cut it out and tacked it above the mantelpiece. I was in my second year at UCL, and I still had dreams. I was going to be a scientist, and go on expeditions, and discover the origins of the universe. Or the secrets of the atom. I wasn't quite sure which.

That's when it hit me: just now, staring at "A Polar Scene". I thought of the body in the river and I said to myself, Jack, you *idiot*. This is the only chance you'll ever get. If you turn it down, what's the point of going on? Another year at Marshall Gifford and they'll be fishing *you* out of the Thames.

It's five in the morning and the milk floats are rattling past under my window. I've been up all night and I feel amazing. Cold, hungry, light-headed. But amazing.

I keep seeing old man Gifford's face. "But Miller, this is madness! In a few years you could be Export Supervisor!"

He's right, it is mad. Chuck in a secure job at a time like this? A *safe* job, too. If there is another war, I'd be excused combat.

But I can't think about that now. By the time I get back, there probably *will* be another war, so I can go off and fight. Or if there isn't, I'll go to Spain and fight.

It's odd. I think war is coming, but I can't feel much about it. All I feel is relief that Father isn't alive to see it. He'll never know that he fought the War to End All Wars for nothing.

And as I said, it doesn't seem *real*. For this one year, I'm going to get away from my life. I'm going to see the midnight sun, and polar bears, and seals sliding off icebergs into green water. I'm going to the Arctic.

It's six months till we sail for Norway. I've spent the whole night planning. Working out how soon I can hand in my notice and still survive till July. Going through the Army & Navy Price List, marking up kit. I've drafted a fitness plan and a reading list, because it occurs to me that I don't actually know very much about Spitsbergen. Only that it's a clutch of islands halfway between Norway and the Pole, a bit bigger than Ireland, and mostly covered in ice.

When I started this journal, I was convinced I wouldn't be going on the expedition. Now I'm writing because I need to record the exact moment when I decided to do this. The body in the river. If it hadn't been for that poor bastard, I wouldn't be going.

So thank you, nameless corpse, and I hope you're at peace now, wherever you are.

I am going to the Arctic.

That picture above the mantelpiece, I've just noticed. There's a seal in the foreground. All these years and I

11

thought it was a wave, but actually it's a seal. I can make out its round, wet head emerging from the water. Looking at me.

I think I'll take that as a good omen.

CHAPTER
TWO

I didn't want to write anything more until we reached Norway, for fear of tempting fate. I was convinced that something would happen to scupper the expedition. It nearly did.

Two days before we were due to set off, Teddy Wintringham's father died. He left a manor in Sussex, "some village property", a tangle of trusts and a clutch of dependants. The heir was "most frightfully cut up" (about the expedition, not his father), but although he felt "absolutely ghastly" about it, it simply wouldn't do for him to be gone a year, so he had to scratch.

The others actually talked about cancelling. Would it be "responsible" to go without a medico? I had a job keeping my temper. To hell with "responsible"; we're young, fit men! Besides, if anyone gets sick, there's a doctor at Longyearbyen — and that's only, what, two days away from camp.

It turns out that Hugo and Gus agreed with me, because when we took a vote, only tub-of-lard Algie voted against. And since he's the last person to stick his neck out, he backed down as soon as he realised he was outnumbered.

Afterwards, I went back to my room and threw up. Then I got out my map of Spitsbergen. The map calls it

"Svalbard" because that's its new name, but everyone uses the old one, which is also the name of the biggest island. That's where we're going. I've marked our base camp in red. There, in the far north-east corner, on the tip of that promontory. Gruhuken. Gru-huken. I think "huken" means hook, or headland. Not sure about "Gru".

There's nothing there. Just a name on the map. I love that. And I love the fact that none of the three previous expeditions ever camped there. I want it to be ours.

Everyone was nervous on the train to Newcastle. Lots of hearty jokes from the 'varsity that I couldn't follow. Gus tried to explain them, but it only made me feel more of an outsider. In the end he gave up, and I went back to staring out of the window.

We had an awful crossing in the mail packet to Bergen and up the Norwegian coast, and Algie and Hugo were seasick. Hugo vomited neatly, like a cat, but fat Algie spattered all over our luggage. Gus mopped up after him without complaint; apparently they've been best friends since prep school. Thank God I've got a cast-iron stomach, so at least I didn't have to worry about being sick. But every night as I rolled in my berth, I dreamed I was back at Marshall Gifford. Every morning I woke up soaked in sweat, and had to tell myself it wasn't true.

And now here we are at Tromsø. Tromsø, where Amundsen took off in his flying boat nine years ago and was never seen again. Tromsø: three hundred miles north of the Arctic Circle. My first encounter with the midnight sun.

Only there isn't any. The gentle, penetrating mizzle hasn't let up in days. Tromsø is a nice little fishing town: wooden houses painted red, yellow and blue, like a child's building blocks, and I'm told that it's backed by beautiful snowy mountains. I wouldn't know, I've never seen them.

But I don't care. I love everything about this place, because it isn't London. Because I'm free. I love the clamour of the gulls and the sea slapping at the harbour walls. I love the salty air and the smell of tar. Above all, I love this soft, watery, never-ending light. Hugo says this is probably how Catholics imagine purgatory, and maybe he's right. There's no dawn and no dusk. Time has no meaning. We've left the real world, and entered a land of dreams.

Of course, the gulls mew day and night, as they can't tell the difference, but I don't even mind that. I'm writing this with the curtains open on the strange, pearly "night" that is no night. I can't sleep. The expedition is really happening. Everything we do, *everything*, only makes it more real.

I was right about Gus being a *Boy's Own* hero. He doesn't have that square jaw or those clear blue eyes for nothing; he takes being Expedition Leader seriously. The funny thing is, I don't find that annoying; maybe because I get the sense that the expedition matters almost as much to him as it does to me.

Months ago, he engaged the British vice consul here as our agent. He's called Armstrong and he's been busy. He's chartered a ship to take us to Gruhuken. He's bought coal, boats and building materials for our cabin, and had them dropped on the coast, to be picked up later. He's bought a sledge and a team of dogs, and got us permission from the Norwegian Government to overwinter. He's even engaged rooms for us at the Grand Hotel — which *is* actually quite grand.

He's also been urging us to have a word with our skipper, Mr Eriksson, who's got some sort of problem with Gruhuken. Apparently he doesn't think it's "right" for a camp. I'm glad to say that none of us is inclined to discuss the matter with Mr Eriksson, thank you very much, and Gus has quietly made him aware of that. We chose Gruhuken after weeks of poring over the surveys from the previous expeditions. It's not for some Norwegian sealer to mess up our plans. As long as he gets us there by August, so that we can set up the second camp on the icecap before the winter, he can consider his job done.

26th July

The amounts of money we're spending, it's frightening!

In London, Hugo was in charge of drumming up finance, and I must say he's done a good job. He has an almost lawyerly ability to persuade people, and he's cadged discounts from firms hoping for endorsements, and talked the War Office into donating my wireless equipment for free. Everything else is coming out of the Expedition Fund, which is made up of grants from the University Exploration Club, the Royal Geographical Society, and "individual subscribers" (I suspect aunts);

total: £3,000. Gus says we have to "be careful", which is why we're buying most things in Norway, as it's so much cheaper there; but "being careful" doesn't mean the same to him as it does to me.

In Newcastle we bought what we wouldn't be able to get in Norway: egg powder, Fry's eating chocolate, and — since Norway is "dry" — spirits, tobacco and cigarettes. That's when I learned that the rich have different priorities. Third-class passages to Norway; then a crate of Oxford marmalade, and two bottles of champagne for Christmas.

In Tromsø, we've been like children let loose in a sweetshop. Mountains of jam, tea, coffee, flour, yeast, sugar and cocoa; tinned fruits, dried vegetables, butter (*not* margarine; I don't think the others have ever tasted it), and crates of something called "pemmican", which is a kind of preserved meat: one grade for us, another for the dogs.

And our kit! Long silk underclothing (*silk!*), woollen stockings, mittens, mufflers and sweaters; kapok waistcoats, corduroys and waterproof Shackleton trousers; "*anoraks*" (a kind of wind jacket with the hood attached), rubber boots, horsehide gauntlets and balaclava helmets. For the coldest weather, we've bought leather boots made by the Lapps, well tarred, and turned up at the toe. You buy them much too big, so you can stuff them with straw when the time comes.

Hugo got the outfitter to take a photo of us in our winter gear. We look like real explorers. Algie's as round as an Eskimo; Hugo and I are both thin and dark, as if

17

we've spent months on hard rations; and Gus could be Scandinavian, maybe Amundsen's younger brother.

But it was buying the rest of our equipment that really brought home to me what we'll be taking on. Tents, sleeping bags, ammunition, *reindeer hides* (as groundsheets, apparently). Above all, a formidable pile of paraffin lamps, headlamps and electric torches. It's hard to believe now, in this endless daylight, but there'll come a time when it's always dark. Thinking of that gives me a queer flutter in my stomach. In a way, I can't wait. I want to see if I can take it.

Not that we'll be roughing it at Gruhuken. We've got a crate of books and a gramophone player, and even a set of Royal Doulton china, donated by Algie's mama. Sometimes I wish it wasn't going to be quite so easy. It's as if we'll be playing at being in the Arctic. Not the real thing at all.

Talking of the real thing, in the morning, we're joining our ship, the *Isbjørn*, and its skipper, Mr Eriksson. He's a hardened sealer and trapper who's overwintered on Spitsbergen a dozen times. I've never met a trapper, but I've read about them and I know my Jack London. They're the real thing. Battling the elements, shooting seals and polar bears. In Norway, people look up to them as "true hunters". All of which I find a bit daunting.

The books say the golden days of trapping were when Spitsbergen was a no-man's-land. I still can't get over that. The idea that until a few years ago, a wilderness not far from Europe belonged to *no one*: that a man could literally stake his claim wherever he liked, without seeking permission from a living soul. It sounds wonderful. But it came to an end in 1925, when the islands became part of Norway.

The stories they tell of that time! Marauding bears. Lethal accidents on the ice. Men going mad from the dark and the loneliness, murdering each other, shooting themselves.

There's even a name for it. They call it *rar*. Armstrong shrugs it off as a "strangeness" which comes over some people when they winter in the Arctic. He says it's simply a matter of a few odd habits, like hoarding matches or obsessively checking stores. But I know from the books that it's worse than that.

And they talk of something called *Ishavet kaller*, which seems to be an extreme form of *rar*. It means "the Arctic calls". That's when a trapper walks off a cliff for no reason.

One time, not long ago, they found four men on Barents Island starved to death in their cabin, despite having piles of ammunition and guns in perfect working order. The man who wrote the book says they'd been too frightened to leave the cabin — *for terror of the deadness beyond*. It makes a good story. But how could he possibly know?

Rar. Ishavet kaller. Cabin fever. Nerve strain. I can understand why it used to happen in the old days, when men were utterly cut off, but it's different now. We'll have a gramophone and the wireless.

And maybe, after all, that's for the best. I mean, compared to those trappers, we're amateurs. Algie's the only one who's ever been to the Arctic, and that was only six weeks' shooting in Greenland. No sense biting off more than we can chew.

27th July, the Isbjørn, somewhere in the Norwegian Sea

I'm writing this in my cabin. *My cabin*. OK, it stinks of seal blubber and it's only slightly bigger than a coffin. But still. The *Isbjørn*'s beautiful, a jaunty little sailing ship, just how I imagine the one in *Moby-Dick* — only with a 50 h.p. Diesel engine that belches greasy black smoke. The ever-accurate Hugo tells me she's a ninety-foot sealing sloop (whatever that means), and that the crow's-nest, three-quarters of the way up her mast, is the mark of a true sealer. Inside, she's mostly hold, with four tiny cabins off the small saloon (I'm in one of these). I don't know where the crew sleeps, or even how many there are, as I can't tell them apart. They're all splendid Nordic types with formidable beards and amazingly clean overalls.

Mysteriously, they don't stink of seal blubber, but everything else does. The rancid, oily smell has soaked into the woodwork. You can taste it in the drinking water. Hugo and Algie are looking green, and I'm feeling a bit queasy myself.

Somehow, we got everything on board, and the crew didn't drop any of my wireless crates. They're safe in the hold, thank God, not on deck with the dogs.

Those bloody dogs. I know we need them for the camp on the icecap, but I wish we didn't. According to

Algie (our self-styled huntsman and dog-driver), Eskimo huskies are the toughest and best able to stand the cold, which is why we had them brought all the way from Greenland. Eight of the brutes: filthy and overexcited after nine weeks cooped up in the holds of various ships.

To the upper classes, dogs are a religion, so Gus, Hugo and Algie already adore ours. They tell me they're "really very friendly" and gave their new masters a rapturous welcome. I wouldn't know, I wasn't there. I don't like dogs and they don't like me.

Gus says this lot will win me over in the end, but I wouldn't bet on it. They look like a pack of wolves. Shaggy, with teeth that can crunch through saucepans, and alarming ice-blue eyes. Cunning, too. While the crew was getting them aboard, one clawed open the bolt on its crate and escaped. After an epic chase round the wharf, it fell in the harbour, where it swam in circles, yowling, until it was rescued. Algie says the only thing that scares a husky is the sea. Well then it shouldn't have fallen in, should it?

I'd assumed they'd be going in the hold, but the others vetoed that as cruel, so they're loose on deck: curled up on coils of rope, or prowling between crates. I'm not looking forward to five days of picking my way through a thicket of fangs.

I read somewhere that in Greenland, if a sledge-driver stumbles in front of his dogs, they eat him alive. Algie says that's rot. But how does he know for sure?

I'm still troubled by what happened, so I'm going to try and get it straight.

We hadn't seen much of the skipper till he joined us for dinner, so to begin with, we were a little intimidated. He looks like a Viking: sharp grey eyes and a grizzled beard. He's got a handshake like a vice, and he calls me "Professor". He calls us all "Professor". I don't know if he's making fun of us or not.

We four sat like schoolboys dining with the headmaster. The saloon's cramped, warm and smelly, with a constant throb of engines, but extremely clean. Dinner was a tasty fish stew, with coffee the way Norwegians like it: viciously strong, with nothing so frivolous as milk or sugar.

Skipper Eriksson is a man's man, all right. Probably a hard drinker when you get to know him, with a fund of dirty jokes. But I like him. I respect him, too. He was born poor. Not middle-class poor like me, but real, grinding, rural poor. He's been a sealer since he was eleven, and has worked his way up to being skipper and part-owner of the *Isbjørn*. To his credit, he treats us with neither envy nor scorn, but simply as rich young "yentlemen" whose mystifying pleasure it is to spend a year in the wild, studying the weather.

The subject of Gruhuken only came up once, and it was Gus, as Expedition Leader, who introduced it. "So, Mr Eriksson," he said towards the end of the meal, "we're delighted that your splendid ship is to be our home all the way to Gruhuken." His tone was polite but firm, and his message was clear. *We mean to go to Gruhuken, and we don't want any objections from you.*

The Norwegian's smile faltered, but he didn't take up the challenge. Dropping his gaze, he rubbed his thumb across his lip. "She is a good ship, *ja*. I hope you will like her."

I exchanged glances with the others, and Gus gave a satisfied nod. Good. That's settled.

But later, while the others were talking, I caught Mr Eriksson watching them. His face was grave. Then his eyes shifted to me. I smiled. He didn't smile back.

Whatever his reservations about Gruhuken, I'm glad he's keeping them to himself, because I don't want to hear them. I don't want anything to get in the way of our plans.

Over cigars (Hugo's diplomatic way of breaking the ice), I'd been planning to ask the skipper what it's like to overwinter in the wilderness, but somehow I couldn't. I had the same feeling I used to get when I was a boy, longing to ask Father about the Great War. I couldn't do it then and I couldn't now, maybe because I sensed that it wouldn't do any good; that he wouldn't tell me what I want to know.

Luckily, fat Algie wasn't nearly so scrupulous. Like a big russet labrador, he simply blundered straight in and asked. And to my surprise, Mr Eriksson readily opened up. Or rather, he seemed to. But I noted that his stories were always about others, never himself.

The best one was about a trapper who was overwintering with a companion in a tiny hut on the coast of North-East Land. Halfway through what Mr Eriksson calls "the dark time", the other man fell sick and died. The trapper couldn't bury him, as the ground was frozen, and he couldn't build a cairn over the body for fear of attracting bears. So instead he simply kept it with him in the hut. Two months with a corpse. Then the spring came, and he was rescued by a passing ship.

When Mr Eriksson finished, there was a respectful silence. "And when they found him," I said at last, "was he — the survivor — was he all right?"

"*Ja*, for sure." Mr Eriksson's tone was brisk.

"But two months . . . How did he manage?"

"Singing songs. Reading his Bible." His gaze skewered mine, and he chuckled. "Not everyone go crazy, Professor."

I flushed. "I only meant it must have been hard."

"Hard? *Ja*." He said it in the Scandinavian way, on an in-breath, which makes it sound oddly like a gasp.

"But what I want to know," said Hugo, leaning forwards and fixing the Norwegian with his dark, inquisitorial gaze, "is *why*? Why put yourself through it when the risks are so enormous, and the rewards so uncertain?"

Eriksson shrugged. "Some men are poor. Some have troubles. Some want respect."

"What about you?" I said. "Why did you do it?"

His brow furrowed. "*Ach*, I don't know. In the open country a man can breathe with both lungs."

Gus nodded. "And I suppose it must have been even better when it didn't belong to anyone."

24

"No-man's-land," I said. I asked Mr Eriksson if he missed that time.

That's when it happened. The Norwegian paused with his mug halfway to his lips and looked at me. His features went stiff. His small eyes drained of expression. It was unnerving. We all noticed it, even Algie.

Unsettled, I wondered if the skipper was angry. I had the distinct impression that he suspected me of some hidden meaning.

"I only meant the freedom of it," I said quickly. "To be able to go where you please. Do what you please. That — surely that must have been wonderful?"

Mr Eriksson dropped his gaze. He shook his head. "No."

An awkward silence.

Then Hugo turned the conversation, and shortly afterwards, Mr Eriksson set down his mug and went back to the bridge.

I've described this in detail, because I'm trying to make sense of it. I like the skipper. The last thing I want is to offend him. But for the life of me, I can't see how I have.

Did I touch some raw nerve? Or is it simply that he thinks we're fools: crazy young "yentlemen" out of our depth? Maybe that's why he told the story about the trapper. A warning.

But we're *not* ill-prepared, and we're *not* out of our depth.

And no matter how many stories he tells, I'm not afraid of what's in store for us at Gruhuken. I'm looking forward to it.

CHAPTER
THREE

Now I know I'm really in the Arctic.

Until this morning, it's been two days of rain, followed by fog. We kept bundling up and going on deck, but there was nothing to see except grey sky melting into grey sea. We haven't seen much of Mr Eriksson, either. Since dinner that first night, he's had most of his meals in his cabin, and on deck he seems preoccupied. The sea has been calm, with only a gentle swell, and Hugo and Algie have found their sea legs. We've got used to the smell of blubber, and no one's been sick; but we've all been a bit subdued.

And now — the ice.

According to Mr Eriksson, it's a belt of drift ice a few miles wide, and nothing to worry about; the *Isbjørn* can take it in her stride. But that doesn't begin to convey what it's like.

It was eerie, peering through the fog at the sea turned white. Huge, jagged floes like pieces of an enormous jigsaw, dotted with pools of meltwater, intensely blue. I hadn't expected it to be so beautiful. It brought a lump to my throat.

Mr Eriksson cut the engines, and I leaned over the side and gazed down at the rocking, jostling shards.

Then I became aware of an odd, rapid popping sound; a brittle crackling, very low, but continuous.

The others came to see what I was looking at, and I said, could they hear it? Hugo said, "Oh, that's just air bubbles in the ice, being popped by the slapping of the waves."

"Sounds as if it's talking to itself," I said.

Hugo shook his head and grinned. Fat Algie goggled at me as if I'd gone mad.

Gus threw me a curious glance. "I was thinking the same thing."

The others drifted away, but Gus and I stayed.

Gus leaned over the edge, his fair hair lifting in the breeze. "Our first ice," he said fondly.

I nodded. "It's OK, isn't it?"

"Oh, yes. It's grand."

"Sorry. That's what I meant."

He sighed. "You know, Jack, sometimes you can be a tad oversensitive."

"Oh, really?"

"Yes, really. I don't care what words you use."

"You might feel differently if you were me."

"Perhaps. But Jack." He turned to me, and his blue eyes were troubled. "Jack, do please believe me. I really *don't* care what words you use, I care what you mean. And doesn't all this" — a sweep of his arm — "make all that irrelevant?"

"It's a bit more complicated than that," I said. "Class matters because money matters."

"I know, but —"

"No you don't. You've got a twenty-five-bedroom house in the West Country and three cars. How can you know? How can you know what it's like to come down in the world, to miss your chance?"

"But you haven't missed your chance."

"Yes I have." Suddenly I was angry. "My family were all right once. Not like yours, but all right. My father was a Classics teacher. He was gassed in the War and couldn't work, so we had to move, and I had to go to a school where they say 'OK' instead of 'grand'. Then he got TB and died, and the Army wouldn't give Mother a pension because he hadn't got TB from being gassed. Then the slump came and I had to give up physics and be a sodding clerk . . ." I broke off.

"I didn't know," said Gus.

"Well you do now. So don't brush it aside as if it doesn't matter."

After that, we didn't talk. Gus stood twisting the signet ring on his little finger, and I felt embarrassed — and furious with myself for blurting things out. What's got into me?

Later
. . . .

All day we've been making our way through the ice. I love it. The purity. The danger.

A man in the crow's-nest calls directions, and Mr Eriksson steers the *Isbjørn* slowly through. At one point, he cut the engine, and some of the crew lowered a boat and went fishing. Others let down a ladder and

28

climbed on to a floe the size of a football pitch, which abutted the hull. While they were filling a barrel with meltwater, the dogs jumped down on to the floe and raced about. We quickly followed.

I couldn't believe it. A few days ago I was in London. Now I'm standing on an ice floe in the Barents Sea.

While the others were playing with the dogs, I wandered off to the edge. According to the ship's thermometer, it's only a couple of degrees below freezing, but it was colder on the ice. My breath rasped in my throat. I felt the skin of my face tighten. And for the first time in my life, I was aware of cold as a menace. A physical threat. The ice was solid beneath my boots — and yet, I thought, a few inches below me, there's water so cold that if I fell in, I'd be dead within minutes. And the only thing that's keeping me away from it is . . . more water.

Moving closer to the edge, I peered down. The water was glassy green, extraordinarily clear. I experienced the feeling I sometimes get when I'm on a bridge or a railway platform. Rationally, you know that you've no intention of stepping off the bridge or the platform — or this ice floe — but you're aware that you *could*, and that the only thing stopping you is your will.

Something slid through the water and vanished under the ice. I thought of all the lives hunting in the dark beneath my feet.

As I write this, it's nearly midnight, and we're still not through the ice. I can feel each turn the ship makes. The shudder of impact, the change in the engine as we reach a clear patch, the subdued roar as we push the smaller floes aside. I think of those great shards rocking, talking to themselves.

I suppose what Gus was trying to say is that here in the Arctic, class doesn't matter. I think he's wrong about that, class always matters.

But maybe up here it doesn't matter so much.

31st July, Spitsbergen

By morning we were clear of the ice, and Mr Eriksson said we'd already passed the Sørkapp, the southernmost tip of Spitsbergen. But the fog wouldn't let us see. All day we huddled on deck, waiting for a glimpse. It got colder. We kept running down to our cabins to pull on more clothes. And still nothing.

Some time after midnight, our patience was finally rewarded. The fog thinned, and although the sky remained overcast, the midnight sun behind the clouds cast a subdued grey radiance on an alien wilderness.

The Dutch whalers of the sixteenth century gave it the right name. Spitsbergen: the pointed mountains. I saw jagged peaks streaked with snow, looming over the mouth of a fjord where the black water was mirror-smooth, and dotted with icebergs. Further in, a vast, tormented glacier spilled into the sea. And all so incredibly still.

Hugo was shaking his head in disbelief. Even Algie was impressed.

Gus said quietly, "Do you realise, it's nearly one in the morning?"

I tried to speak but I couldn't. It was utterly unlike anything I'd ever seen. It was — intimidating. No, that's not the right word. It made me feel irrelevant. It made humanity irrelevant. I wonder if Gruhuken will be like this?

Hugo, the keen glaciologist, asked Mr Eriksson to head into the fjord to get nearer the glacier, and we craned our necks at fissured walls of ice and caverns of mysterious blue. From deep within came weird creaks and groans, as if a giant were hammering to get out. Then came a noise like a rifle shot, and a huge segment of ice crashed into the sea, sending up spouts of water, and a wave that rocked the ship. Shattered ice turned the sea a milky pale-green. The hammering went on. Now I know why people used to believe that Spitsbergen was haunted.

But as we headed north up the coast, I realised that despite all my reading, I'd made the classic mistake of imagining the Arctic as an empty waste. I'd thought that since it's too far north for trees, there wouldn't be much else except rocks. Maybe a few seals and sea-birds, but nothing like this. I never expected so much life.

Great flocks of gulls perching on icebergs, rising in flurries, diving after fish. An Arctic fox trotting over a green plain with a puffin flapping in its jaws. Reindeer raising antlered heads to watch us pass. Walruses rocking on the waves; one surfaced right beneath me with an explosive, spraying *huff!* and regarded me with a phlegmatic brown eye. The sleek heads of seals bobbed on the surface, observing us with the same curiosity with which we observed them. Algie shot one, but it sank before the men could retrieve it. He would have shot a reindeer, too, if they weren't protected by law. He seems to enjoy killing things.

We passed a cliff thronged with thousands of sea-birds. Gulls screamed, and the rockfaces echoed with the strange, rattling groans of black birds with stubby wings which Gus said were guillemots. He said what I'd taken for gulls were kittiwakes, and that the Vikings believed that their cries were the wails of lost souls.

Many of the beaches are littered with driftwood, borne from Siberia by the Atlantic current, and weathered to silver. And bones: huge, arching whale ribs many decades old. According to Mr Eriksson, we're so far north that "dead things" last for years.

But there are other, less picturesque remains. Abandoned mines, and the broken-down cabins of prospectors long gone. In an inlet I saw a post rising from a cairn of rocks, with a plank nailed across the top. I assumed it was a grave, but one of the seamen told me it was a claim sign.

I don't like these human relics. I don't want to be reminded that Spitsbergen has been exploited for hundreds of years. Whalers, miners, trappers, even tourists. Thank God there's only a handful of tiny settlements, and we're not going near any of them.

Just before dinner, Mr Eriksson spotted something on an island, and brought the ship in closer.

At first I couldn't see anything except a pebbly beach strewn with driftwood. Then I made out the blotchy, pinkish-brown carcass of a walrus, lying on its back. Its yellow tusks jutted upwards, and its body looked curiously deflated, like a giant, kicked-in football. Then I realised why. Something had gnawed a hole in its belly and eaten it from the inside.

The polar bear rose from behind a boulder and stretched its long neck to catch our scent.

It was my first glimpse of the king of the Arctic. But this was nothing like the snowy giant of my imagination. Blood and blubber had stained its pelt a dirty brown; its head and neck were almost black. I couldn't see its eyes, but I sensed them. Until that moment, I've never felt like prey. Never been so intensely watched by a creature who would kill me if it got the chance. I stared at it, and I felt death staring back.

A shot rang out. The bear turned its head. Algie took aim again. Before he could shoot, the bear had ambled out of sight.

Kill or be killed. That's what it comes down to. And yet somehow, I don't find that appalling. There's truth in it. A kind of stark beauty.

I think that's what the Arctic means to me. I think that up here, I'll be able to "breathe with both lungs", as Mr Eriksson says: to see clearly for the first time in years. Right through to the heart of things.

CHAPTER
FOUR

Disaster. Hugo tripped on a coil of rope and broke his leg.

Everyone went into emergency mode, very calm and stiff upper lip. "Buck up, old chap, we'll soon set you to rights." The consequences were too huge to be voiced out loud.

The first mate splinted the leg, and we carried Hugo down to his cabin. Mr Eriksson, his face inscrutable, turned the ship about, and set course for Longyearbyen.

The first mate did what he could for Hugo, and then Gus, Algie and I squeezed into his cabin and tried to convince him that he hadn't let us down and endangered the whole expedition.

"Stupid, stupid, bugger bugger *bugger!*" He pounded the mattress with his fists. His dark hair was plastered to his temples, his cheeks flushed after a dose of cocaine from the medicine chest.

"It's not your fault," Gus said tonelessly.

"'Course it isn't!" Algie robustly agreed.

I chimed in too late, and Hugo noticed. I didn't care. I was furious with him.

Algie gave an uneasy laugh. "We seem to be jinxed, don't we? First Teddy, now Hugo."

34

"Thank you for stating the blindingly obvious," said Gus.

For a moment, no one spoke. Then Hugo said, "Right. Here's what we do. You'll drop me off at Longyearbyen, where I'll get myself patched up, and wire the sponsors and find a berth on the next boat home. And you chaps," he lifted his chin, "will carry on without me."

Silence. No one wanted to admit that they'd been thinking the same thing.

Perplexed, Algie ran a hand through his carroty hair. "But — you're our glacier fellow. Who'll man the camp on the icecap?"

"We'll have to scrap it, of course," snapped Gus.

"What?" cried Algie. "But the dogs . . ."

"Are now completely unnecessary," said Hugo. "God, Algie, you can be dim."

"I don't understand," said Algie. "What do we do about the dogs?"

Gus flung up his arms.

"It seems to me," I said, "that we'd be better off without them. I asked Mr Eriksson if we could sell them in Longyearbyen, but he said the mine manager's already got a team. He said . . ." I hesitated. "He thinks we should put them down."

A chorus of outrage. How could I even contemplate such a thing? The dogs would be useful in all sorts of ways: taking Algie about on his geological survey, warning us of bears. Suggestion emphatically overruled.

"Right, then, we're agreed," said Hugo, suppressing a wince as he shifted position. "I go home, and you three carry on without me. With the dogs. Yes?"

Nobody wanted to be the first to agree.

We left poor Hugo an hour ago in the "Sykehus" at Longyearbyen. Tomorrow he'll board the tourist yacht and head back to Tromsø. I'll miss him. I think we could have been friends. I wish it was fat Algie who'd broken his leg.

Hugo didn't want us to stay, which was a relief, because in Longyearbyen I felt as out of place as the tourists from that yacht.

God, what a dump. A ramshackle settlement of some five hundred souls, it's all that's left of the great Arctic "coal rush". A few decades ago, a clutch of prospectors reported huge deposits, and greed took over. Nations scrambling to stake claims, companies sprouting like mushrooms, raising millions on expectation alone. Most have gone bankrupt, or were bought for a song by the Norwegians, who now run what remains.

According to the books, Longyearbyen boasts electricity and water piped from a glacier, as well as a billiards hall and a bathhouse. What I saw were ugly miners' barracks cowering at the feet of stark grey mountains. A cable railway strung along their flanks like a grimy necklace, its buckets dumping coal on the jetty in clouds of black dust. A single street strewn with rubbish and mobbed by screaming gulls. A wooden church and a cluster of grave-markers on a hill.

On our way back to the ship, we passed a group of miners heading for "town". One turned his head and stared at me. His face was black with soot, his eyes angry and inflamed. He looked scarcely human.

Capable of anything. I felt obscurely menaced. And ashamed.

It feels wrong that there should be such places on Spitsbergen. I'm glad Gruhuken is far away from all this. I don't want it sullied.

2nd August, near Cape Mitra, north-west Spitsbergen

First Hugo, now this. *Damn* Eriksson. He's cast a pall over the whole expedition — and for what? He hasn't even given us a reason.

This morning, Algie and I were on deck when Gus called us down to the saloon.

We knew at once that something was wrong. Eriksson sat in stony silence, his hands spread flat on the table. Gus' face was set, his blue eyes glassy with anger.

"Ah, gentlemen." He greeted us in clipped tones. "It seems that Mr Eriksson here refuses to take us to Gruhuken."

We stared at the skipper. He wouldn't meet our eyes.

"He says," Gus went on, "that he'll take us as far as Raudfjord, but no further . . ."

"But that's forty miles short!" cried Algie.

". . . and he says," continued Gus, "that these were always his orders. That he's never heard any mention of Gruhuken."

The blatancy of the Norwegian's lie astonished me. And he didn't back down. In fact, he put up quite a fight. He insisted that he'd been chartered to take us to

Raudfjord and no further. We said this was nonsense, our goal had always been Gruhuken. He said there was good camping on Raudfjord. We pointed out that Raudfjord has no icecap, and we'd hardly have gone to the trouble of bringing a sledge and eight dogs if we didn't need them. He said he knew nothing of that. His ship had been chartered for Raudfjord, and to Raudfjord she would go.

We reached stalemate. Algie muttered something irrelevant about legal action. Gus seethed. The Norwegian crossed his arms and glowered.

Behind his granite demeanour, I sensed unhappiness. He hated reneging on his charter. So why was he doing it?

Before I could say anything, Gus placed both palms on the table and leaned towards the skipper. His usual genial manner was gone. In its place I saw the assurance which comes from generations of command. "Now look here, Eriksson," he said. "You will carry out the job for which you were hired. You will take us to Gruhuken — and there's an end of it!"

Poor Gus. Maybe that works on his father's estate, but not with a man like Eriksson. The Norwegian sat like a boulder, immovable.

I decided it was my turn. "Mr Eriksson," I said. "Do you remember our first night on board? I asked you why you chose to overwinter on Spitsbergen, and you said it's because there a man can breathe with both lungs. I took that to mean that you felt free. Free to make your own decisions. Was I right?"

He didn't reply. But I had his attention.

"Don't you see it's the same for us?" I went on. "We thought long and hard about where to site our camp, and we chose Gruhuken. We chose it. We made a decision."

"You don't know what you are doing," he growled.

"Now look here," cried Gus.

"Oh, I say!" exclaimed Algie at the same time.

Without taking my eyes from Eriksson's, I signed them to silence. "What do you mean by that?"

"You don't know," he repeated.

"Then tell me," I urged. "Come now, you're an honourable man. And yet you've gone back on your word. Why? Why don't you want to take us to Gruhuken? What's wrong with it?"

His face darkened. He glared at me.

For a moment I thought he was going to tell me. Then he leapt to his feet and struck the table with both fists. "*Helvedes fand!* As you *wish*! To Gruhuken we go!"

3rd August, off Gruhuken

There's some drift ice in the bay, but also plenty of open water, and Mr Eriksson has dropped anchor a hundred yards from the beach. We wanted to go ashore and explore, but he said it was too late, and the crew was tired. After yesterday's row, we thought it best to humour him.

After dinner, I went on deck and listened to the ice talking to itself. I fancy it sounds different from the ice we encountered further south. Sterner, harsher. But that's only my imagination.

We had a clear run up the coast and round the north-west cape, although the weather remained overcast and foggy. As we headed east, our anticipation grew. Only a few miles left to go. Gus and Algie leaned over the side, counting off landmarks on the map. I went to the wheelhouse to make one last attempt with the skipper.

"Mr Eriksson," I began, with a poor attempt at geniality.

"Professor," he replied without taking his eyes from the sea.

"I don't wish to offend you," I said carefully. "And I'm not suggesting that you haven't been straight with us. But I'd count it a favour if you'd tell me, man to man, why you don't want to take us to Gruhuken."

Still watching the waves, the Norwegian adjusted course. For a moment his glance flicked sideways to me. Something in his expression told me he was wondering if I could be trusted.

"Please," I said. "All I want is the truth."

"Why?"

I was startled. "Well . . . isn't it obvious? We'll be there a year. If there's some problem, we need to know about it."

"It's not always good to know," he said quietly.

"I'm — not sure I agree with you. I think it's always best to know the truth."

He gave me another odd look. Then he said, "Some places . . . they make bad luck."

"What?" I was taken aback. "What do you mean?"

"Gruhuken. It's . . . bad luck. Things happen there."

"What things?"

"Bad things."

"But what? Tricky currents in the bay? Bad weather off the icecap? What?"

He chewed his moustache. "There are worse things."

The way he said that. As if he couldn't bear to think of it.

For a moment I was shaken. Then I said, "But Mr Eriksson. Surely you don't believe that a place — a mere pile of rocks — can make bad things happen?"

"I didn't say that."

"Then what?"

Another silence.

Exasperated, I blew out a long breath. That was my mistake. His face closed and I knew that I'd lost him.

Shouts from the deck. Gus and Algie were beaming and waving at me. "Look, Jack, *look!*"

While I'd been talking to the skipper, the weather had undergone one of those sudden Arctic reversals. The clouds had lifted. The fog had cleared.

That first sight of it. Like a blow to the heart. The desolation. The beauty.

A fierce sun blazed in a sky of astonishing blue. Dazzling snow-capped mountains enclosed a wide bay dotted with icebergs. The water was as still as glass, mirroring the peaks. At the eastern end of the bay, tall cliffs the colour of dried blood were thronged with seabirds, their clamour muted by distance. At the western end, shining pavements of pewter rock sloped down to the sea, and a stream glinted, and a tiny, ruined hut huddled among boulders. The charcoal beach was littered with silver driftwood and the giant ribs of whales. Behind it, greenish-grey slopes rose towards the harsh white glitter of the icecap.

Despite the cries of gulls, there was a stillness about it. A great silence. And God, that *light*! The air was so clear I felt I could reach out and touch those peaks, snap off a chunk of that icecap. Such purity. It was like heaven.

For a moment, I couldn't speak.

I turned to Mr Eriksson. "Is that . . ."

He nodded and sucked in his breath, like a gasp. "*Ja*. Gruhuken."

CHAPTER
FIVE

7th August, Gruhuken
....

Our fourth day at Gruhuken. I've been too exhausted
to write.

This morning we finished unloading the ship. That
meant lowering eighty tons of supplies (and dogs) into
the boats and rowing them ashore; except for the fuel
drums, which we floated into the shallows. I had an
anxious time with my wireless crates — if anything gets
wet, it'll be damaged beyond repair — but thank God,
they made it OK. Then I had to protect them from
the dogs, who were racing about, christening things.
And when a husky is loose, it eats whatever it finds:
wind-proofs, rucksacks, tents. It wasn't long before Gus
and Algie saw sense and tied the brutes to stakes. At
first they complained with ear-shattering yowls, then
they realised it was hopeless and settled down.

I've enjoyed the hard work after being cooped up on
the *Isbjørn*. Every "night" — these strange white nights
that I still find magical — Mr Eriksson and the crew go
back to the ship to sleep, but we're keen to take
possession of Gruhuken, so we've pitched our Pyramid
tent on the beach, at the head of the bay. Our
reindeer-hide groundsheets are supremely comfortable,
and not even the seabirds keep us awake.

We've been so busy that at times I've hardly noticed our surroundings. But sometimes I'll pause and look about, and then I'm sharply aware of all the busy creatures — men, dogs, birds — and behind them the stillness. Like a vast, watching presence.

It's a pristine wilderness. Well, not quite pristine. I was a bit put out to learn that there have been others here before us. Gus found the ruins of a small mine on the slopes behind camp; he brought back a plank with what looks like a claim, roughly painted in Swedish. To make the beach safe for the dogs, we had to clear a tangle of wire and gaffs and some large rusty knives, all of which we buried under stones. And there's that hut, crouched among the boulders in a blizzard of bones.

Gus asked Mr Eriksson about it. "So were there trappers here too? Or was it the miners who left all the bones?"

Mr Eriksson sucked in his breath. "*Ja.*"

Gus raised his eyebrows. "Well, which?"

The Norwegian hesitated. "Trapper first. Miners later."

"And after them, no one," I said. "Not until us."

Mr Eriksson did not reply.

I'm glad to say that relations with him have improved, and he and his crew have worked like demons to help us set up camp; almost, Gus remarked, as if they've a deadline to meet.

And maybe they have. With every day that passes, the midnight sun dips nearer the horizon. In a week, on the 16th, it'll disappear for the first time, and we'll experience our first brief night. Mr Eriksson calls it "first dark". Algie's planning a little ceremony involving whisky to usher it in, but Mr Eriksson disapproves. He seems to think we shouldn't joke about such things.

I've told the others what he said about Gruhuken being unlucky. Gus was briskly dismissive, and Algie said I shouldn't indulge the man's penchant for superstition. Secretly, though, I think they were relieved that it wasn't worse. I feel better, too. Now it's dealt with. Out in the open.

This morning, after the last crate was brought ashore, the *Isbjørn* set off on the forty-mile trip to collect our boats, coal, and the materials for the cabin. It's good to be on our own, a sort of dress rehearsal. And it's given us a chance to explore.

Leaving the dogs tied to their stakes, Algie took his rifle and headed off to hunt, while Gus and I went for a wander to the bird cliffs at the eastern end of the bay.

The weather has been perfect since we arrived, and this was another brilliant, windless day; surprisingly warm in the sun, only just below freezing. The sea was a vivid blue, mirroring the mountains, and out in the bay, I spotted three bearded seals basking on ice floes. I took deep breaths of the clean, salty air, and it went to my head like wine.

Nearer the cliffs, the smell of guano took over. We scrambled among the rocks, Gus pausing now and then to identify yellow Arctic poppies and brilliant green clumps of saxifrage. He's fascinated by nature, and likes pointing things out to me, the ignorant physicist. I don't mind. I quite enjoy it.

The cliffs echoed with the guillemots' rattling groans. Craning my neck, I saw the sky speckled black with birds, like dirty snow. Thousands more perched on ledges. In the shadow of the cliffs the dark-green water was dotted with white feathers. Among them paddled guillemot chicks. Fluffy and flightless, they rode the waves uttering high, piercing cries.

"Poor little scraps," said Gus. "They spend their first three weeks on a ledge, facing the wall. Then they jump off, and if they're lucky they hit the water and swim out to sea with their parents."

"If they're lucky," I remarked. I'd just seen a gull swoop down and swallow a chick whole.

"Not much of a life, is it?" said Gus. "Three weeks with your beak jammed against a rock, then you jump off and get eaten."

A lone chick was bobbing on the swell, peeping. Maybe it'd got separated from its parents, or maybe they'd been taken by the Arctic foxes which haunt the feet of the cliffs like small grey ghosts.

As we made our way round the headland, we heard the distant report of Algie's rifle. We watched a big, thuggish gull bullying a guillemot into disgorging its fish. Gus found a reindeer skull, and showed me its worn-down teeth. He said it would have died of starvation, albeit with a full stomach, as it could no longer chew its food. Sitting on the rocks, we basked in the sun, and I thought about the beauty and cruelty around me.

Without preamble, Gus said, "The other day, I didn't express myself very well. What I was trying to say is that I don't think you've missed your chance."

I felt myself going red.

"What I mean," he went on, "is that although your family had a hard time of it, that needn't drag you down, too."

"It already has," I muttered.

"I don't accept that. You're here. This is a new beginning. Who knows what it'll lead to?"

"That's easy for you to say," I retorted.

"But Jack —"

"Gus, leave it! I came out here to get away from my life, not rake it all up. OK?"

I'd spoken more sharply than I intended, and there was an uncomfortable silence. I shredded a clump of Arctic poppies. Gus counted the tines on the reindeer's antlers.

Then he said, "Back in London, did you really not have any friends?"

I shrugged. "Everyone I knew at UCL was doing further degrees. Why would I want to see them? And I'd got nothing to say to the lads at Marshall Gifford. So I just thought sod it, I'll go it alone."

His lip curled. "You're so extreme."

"No I'm not."

"Yes you are. How many people do you know who've spent seven years entirely on their own?"

"Well, since I don't *know* any people, the answer is none."

He laughed. "That's what I mean! Extreme!"

I bit back a smile.

"And after all that, to end up stuck in a tent with Algie and me." He hesitated. "Tell me honestly. Is it a strain?"

I threw away the poppies and looked at him. Sunlight glinted in his golden hair and lit the strong, clean planes of his face. He wasn't merely good-looking. His features had a chiselled purity that made me think of Greek heroes. I wondered what it must be like to be so handsome. Surely it would affect the behaviour of everyone around you, always?

And more powerful even than his looks, he seemed genuinely to want to know how I was getting on.

"Honestly?" I said. "It's not as bad as I expected."

On the way back, a fulmar glided overhead, so low that I heard the hiss of air beneath its wings. Fulmars are serene grey seabirds which Gus says are first cousins of the albatross. I watched this one skim the waves till it was out of sight. As we headed past the cliffs, I heard that guillemot chick, still peeping. I wished something would eat it and get it over with.

At camp, we found Algie in high spirits. He'd made his way west into the next fjord, where he'd come upon a spit of land "crammed with eider ducks". He'd shot five, and on his return he'd bagged a seal, which he'd hacked to pieces and fed to the dogs. Judging by the amount of blood spattered over the rocks, it had been a big seal, and Algie is a messy butcher.

For dinner we roasted the ducks on a driftwood fire, having (on advice from the ship's cook) removed the fishy-smelling skin. They were the best thing I've ever tasted. We washed up in sand and seawater, then lay about, smoking and drinking whisky. We had a long discussion about whether Amundsen was a greater

48

explorer than Scott, and where did Shackleton fit in, and was Nobile a cad or a decent fellow.

Everyone looks tousled and tanned, and our beards are becoming quite respectable. Algie's is red and fuzzy, like a hedge. Gus' is golden, of course. It suits him inordinately. He says mine makes me look like a pirate. I suppose he means because I'm dark.

I never expected to get on with them like this. OK, sometimes Algie gets on my nerves. He's obtuse and he snores, and takes up so much *space*. But I'm beginning to regard Gus as a friend.

He's quite persuasive, too, is Gus. All that talk about new beginnings. I nearly believed him. It hurt. Like pulling off a scab.

I'm writing this in our tent. Outside it's minus five, but in here, with our eider-down sleeping bags and Gus' fur motoring rug on top, it's quite snug. The tent's green canvas walls are softly aglow in the white Arctic night. There's an occasional yelp from the dogs, but they're tethered a hundred yards away and full of seal, so it's not too bad. I can hear the little waves sucking at the shingle, and the muted cries of seabirds. And now and then there's a crack as an iceberg breaks apart in the bay.

The day after tomorrow, the *Isbjørn* is due back, and we'll start building our cabin.

I never expected this, but I feel at home here. I love Gruhuken. I love the clarity and the desolation. Yes, even the cruelty. Because it's true. It's part of life.

I'm happy.

A strange day. Not altogether good.

After breakfast we decided to take a proper look at Gruhuken's ruins, so that when the *Isbjørn* returns, we'll know what needs clearing away. To my annoyance, Algie brought the dogs. (So far, I've managed to ignore them, and they've sensed my dislike and given me a wide berth.)

Another bright day, almost hot in the sun as we climbed the slopes to inspect the ruined mine — Gus and me striding ahead, Algie puffing in the rear. I was relieved to see that there isn't much left of the mine. A rusty tramcar, a stack of tracks, a few hollows blasted from the rocks.

"No cabins," remarked Algie.

"I asked Eriksson about that," said Gus. "He says they were buried in a rockslide."

Algie grimaced. "Poor chaps."

"Oh, the miners weren't in them. But it was the last straw, and they abandoned the place."

"What do you mean, the last straw?" said Algie.

"What does it matter?" I snapped. "They couldn't make a go of it, so they left, and that's that."

"Steady on, old chap," said Algie, turning pink beneath his freckles.

I was damned if I was going to apologise. I hate all this raking up of the past.

Gus the peacemaker suggested that we leave everything as it is, and we wandered down to take a look at the hut among the boulders.

A grim little place, squatting in its drifts of bones. The dogs didn't like it either. They nosed about edgily, then raced off along the beach to investigate our tent. Which meant that Algie and Gus had to chase after them and tie them up. I went along to show willing, but they wisely didn't ask me to help.

When we got back to the hut, Gus, the inveterate biologist, paused to identify the bones. Many are scattered, the disembodied skulls of walruses and reindeer, but others are recognisable skeletons. Gus pointed out foxes, fine and brittle as porcelain; and the big, manlike frames of bears. And smaller ones with short limbs and long toes that look unsettlingly like human hands, which he said are seals.

I tripped over a claim sign lying on the ground. A posh one, of enamelled tin with emphatic capitals punched out in English, German and Norwegian: *PROPERTY OF THE SPITSBERGEN PROSPECT-ING COMPANY OF EDINBURGH. CLAIMED 1905.*

"And now there's nothing left," said Gus, chucking the sign away.

The hut itself was about six feet square. A lean-to, with three walls of driftwood logs built against a large boulder, presumably to save on timber. The roof was still intact, tarpaper dismally flapping, and the door was only two feet high, perhaps to keep in the heat. The side window had been smashed by a marauding bear, but the small one facing the sea was still shuttered. Three paces in front of it stood a driftwood post planted in a cairn of stones. Algie said it was a "bear post", for luring bears to the trapper's gun.

Gus took out his knife and prised the shutter off the front window, loosing a cascade of splintered glass. The old hut exhaled a musty smell of seaweed.

Gus peered in. "I suppose we could use it for a doghouse. What do you think, Algie?"

Algie shrugged. "Bit small. Though it's a pity to waste it." He glanced at me. "Want to take a look inside, Jack?"

I didn't, but I couldn't think of an excuse.

I've never liked confined spaces, and as I crawled in after him, my spirits sank. The cries of gulls fell away. All I could hear was the wind keening in the stovepipe. The smell was thick in my throat: rotten seaweed, and something else. As if something had crawled in here to die.

The walls were black with soot, the ceiling too low to stand without stooping. In one corner, a rusty iron stove squatted on short bowed legs. Against the back wall, a wooden bunk had collapsed beneath a mound of storm-blown debris. Rooting around, Algie found a mildewed reindeer hide and a battered tin plate. He wrinkled his nose. "Beastly. Hopeless for the dogs." He crawled out. I stayed. I don't know why.

For the first time since reaching Gruhuken, I thought about the men who were here before us; who built this hut from logs dragged up from the beach, and lived through the "dark time", and then left, leaving nothing but a tin plate and a blizzard of bones.

What must it have been like? No wireless, maybe not even a companion; at any rate only one, in a hut this size. To know that you're the only human being in all this wilderness.

Moving to the front window, I scraped the broken glass off the frame and poked out my head. No sign of Algie or Gus. The bear post dominated the view. Beyond it the stony beach sloped down to the sea.

Suddenly, I felt desolate. It's hard to describe. An oppression. A wild plummeting of the spirits. The romance of trapping peeled away, and what remained was this. Squalor. Loneliness. It's as if the desperation of those poor men had soaked into the very timber, like the smell of blubber on the *Isbjørn*.

I crawled out quickly, and inhaled great gulps of salty air. I hate all this pawing over ruins. I want Gruhuken to be *ours*. I don't want to be reminded that others were here before.

11th August
....

I know I'm right. Whatever Mr bloody Eriksson says.

The ship got back as scheduled, and we spent two days unloading. Finished today, and would've made a start on the cabin if it hadn't been for him.

While he was away, we'd decided on where to build it. Which took about five minutes, as it's completely bloody obvious: where the old hut is, at the western end of the bay. It's conveniently near the stream, and the boulders give shelter from the winds off the icecap, *and* it's far enough from the bird cliffs to ensure that my radio masts get decent reception.

But oh no, none of that matters to old Eriksson. As far as he's concerned, we need to be *east*, practically under the bloody cliffs. And we should leave the trappers' hut well alone.

"I think that's nonsense," I said. "That hut's no use to man nor beast, it's got to come down."

"No," Eriksson said flatly.

"Why?" said Gus.

Eriksson muttered something about the dogs.

"I told you," Algie said wearily, "it simply won't do for them."

"It won't do for my wirelesses, either," I said.

Eriksson ignored that. "You're leaving the mining ruins alone, you should leave this too."

"The mining ruins aren't in the way," I said. "That hut most definitely is."

"Not if you build the cabin further east," he said — which brought us right back to where we'd started.

It went on for hours. Eventually he was forced to agree that it would be better if we didn't have to trudge the length of the bay to fetch water, but he remained adamant about not touching the hut. Algie gave in first, suggesting we use it as a storehouse. Then Gus conceded that maybe we could build our cabin alongside it. That's when I lost my temper. Did they want to preserve a ruin, or did they want wirelesses that actually work?

But if I'm honest, I want that hut gone because I simply can't bear the thought of it. Some places drag you down, and that's one of them. Maybe it's the poverty and the loneliness: a reminder of what I came here to escape. Maybe I just don't like it.

Anyway, I won.

Next day
....

It's gone, though we had the devil of a job tearing it down. For some reason, none of the crew wanted to touch it, so we had to pay them double; and Eriksson had to have a stern word with them in Norwegian.

They worked in sullen silence and we helped, dragging the timbers away and chopping them up for firewood. Nothing's left of it now, except for the bear post, which Algie told them to leave, as he wants to use it as a flagpole. I pointed out that we haven't got a flag, and he tapped the side of his nose and said, not yet. God, he can be irritating. Why Gus should regard him as his "best pal" I've no idea.

It's been an exhausting day, and we turned in early. Gus and Algie are already asleep. Gus is frowning in his dreams. He looks young and noble, like the first officer over the top at the Somme. Algie is snoring. His thick red lips glisten with spit.

An hour ago, the weather broke, and a freezing wind came howling down from the icecap. It's still blowing, sucking and smacking at the tent. The icebergs are grinding in the bay, and now and then one breaks apart with a crash. Eriksson says that if this wind keeps up, it'll clear them away, so I suppose that's something.

55

This evening after dinner, when it was still calm, we strolled over to admire the site of our cabin. It's perfect. We've even cleared it of most of the bones. But I wish Algie hadn't kept that bloody post. Gruhuken seems to have had a dismal past. I don't want any of it poking through.

And of course, he had to go on about how the wretched thing works. "Apparently, it comes into its own in winter, when the pack ice gets near the coast and brings the bears. They're attracted to tall, standing things, especially with a slab of blubber dangling from the top. So all you've got to do is stay in your cabin with your rifle poking out the window, and wait till a brute comes within range. I confess I'm rather keen to give it a shot."

"Algie old man," said Gus, "I don't think that's on. We don't want bears prowling around camp."

He and Algie wandered off, amicably bickering, and I strolled down to the beach.

Crossing the stream, I found my way on to the rocks. It was nearly midnight, and the great sloping pavements gleamed in that deep, gold, mysterious light. From a distance, they appear to shelve gently into the shallows, but in fact they end in a nasty four-foot drop. The water's deep, and you can see right down to the bottom, to huge green boulders and undulating weeds like drowned hair.

Crouching at the edge, I watched the waves slapping, and the chunks of ice jostling and clinking. I heard that peculiar crackling as it talked to itself.

I thought, if I fell in, I wouldn't be able to climb out. I'd try to swim round to where it's shallower, but the cold would get me long before then.

As I was heading back, a shaft of sunlight struck the bear post. The wood was bleached silver, except for a few charred patches, and some darker blotches which must be blubber stains. I found it hard to believe it was once a tree in some Siberian forest.

On impulse, I drew off my glove and laid my palm against it. It felt smooth and unpleasantly cold. I didn't like it. A killing post.

And yet I think I now understand the impulse which drives men to shoot bears. It isn't for the pelt or the meat or the sport — or not only those things. I think they *need* to do it. They need to kill that great Arctic totem to give them some sense of control over the wilderness — even if that is only an illusion.

Just now, a shadow sped over the tent, and I got such a fright I nearly cried out.

Steady on, Jack. It was only a gull.

The wind is blowing hard, and the dogs are howling. They're restless tonight.

CHAPTER
SIX

The cabin is finished, and we've moved in!

It went up in three days, as everyone worked like Trojans, and it's beautiful. Black all over: walls covered in tarpaper, roof in felt, with the stovepipe poking a little drunkenly from the top, like the witch's hovel in "Hansel and Gretel". The two front windows are such different sizes that they resemble mismatched eyes.

Between them there's a small enclosed porch, above which Gus has nailed a pair of reindeer antlers: a nice baronial touch. If you turn right and go round the corner, you find the outhouse, which Algie pompously calls the lavatory. At the rear, the eastern half of the cabin is backed by a lean-to of packing cases and wire netting for the dogs, while the western half abuts the boulders. The whole cabin is surrounded (except for the doghouse and the boulders) by a boardwalk about two feet wide. When you're inside and someone treads on this, you can hear the footsteps, and feel the floor vibrate — as Algie is all too fond of demonstrating.

My radio masts stand a few feet to the west, and beyond them is the Stevenson screen for the meteorological measurements. We've fenced that in to keep out the dogs, and set a line of posts with ropes slung between them all the way to the porch, as Mr Eriksson says we'll need this in bad weather. The emergency storehouse is way off near the cliffs; and we've planted the dogs' stakes in front of the cabin, so that we can keep an eye on them.

Before we were even half unpacked, I ran a test on my wireless equipment. It works. *Thank God.* My heart was in my mouth as I started the petrol engine for the big transmitter. When the valves began to glow, the sweat was pouring off me.

Shakily, I tapped out our first message to England. It's childish, I know, but I did enjoy impressing the others. See? Good at it, aren't I?

With head-phones in place and the receiver switched on, I took down our first communication from the outside world. *MESSAGE RECEIVED STOP WE HAVE 5 MESSAGES FOR YOU STOP.* Seventeen hundred miles through the ether, and clear as a bell. *The Times* and the RGS; Hugo, sportingly wishing us luck from Tromsø; Algie's girlfriend; Gus' parents and sister. Algie crassly asked why there was nothing for me, so I told him. Parents dead, no siblings, no friends. I think he wishes he hadn't asked.

The small Gambrell transmitter also works perfectly, as does the Eddystone receiver, which I got going in time for the BBC National Programme. George Gershwin is dead, and the Japs have bombed Shanghai. It all seems very far away.

Or it would have done if Algie hadn't blathered on about Mr Hitler needing a jolly good thrashing. Gus told him sharply to shut up. He's like me, he doesn't

59

want to think about another war. He told me the other day that he comes from a line of soldiers stretching back to Crécy, so the whole thing's rather hanging over him. Which you'd have thought Algie would have remembered, as he's known Gus since they were boys.

Still. All that's over now, and we've been settling into our new home.

It's thirty feet by twenty, which sounds a lot, but is actually pretty cramped, as we've got so much equipment. When you enter the porch, you have to squeeze past a tangle of skis, snowshoes, shovels and brooms. Then — and I'm told this will be crucial in winter — you shut the front door *before* you open the one to the hall. (Mr Eriksson calls this the First Rule of the Arctic: always shut one door before opening the next. Especially in a blizzard.)

With that door shut behind you, you're in darkness, because the hall — which is narrow and extends along the frontage — has no window, only gun racks and hooks for waterproofs, and a cupboard which Gus calls his darkroom. There's also a hatch into the roof space, which is our main food store.

Having groped your way down the hall, you open the door to the bunkroom — and *fiat lux*, a window! The bunkroom occupies the eastern end of the cabin, and is mostly bunk, with shelves made of packing cases on the opposite wall. We only needed three bunks, but it was easier to build four. I've got the bottom one at the back. (The one above me is empty; we use it as a dumping ground.) My bunk is nearest the stove in the main room, which is good; but it's got the doghouse directly behind.

From my bunk, you can see straight into the main room, as that doorway has no door. To your right as you go in, there's the stove, water barrel, and shelves which make up the "kitchen" (no sink, of course). The main room is dominated by a big pine table and five chairs, and against the back wall are shelves crammed with books, ammunition, field glasses, microscopes and provisions.

The western end of the cabin, on the site of the old trappers' hut, is my wireless area. It's packed with receivers and transmitters, the Austin engine, and the bicycle generator, which faces the west window, so that I can see my wireless masts. My work bench is at the front, under the north window, overlooking the bear post. As the wireless area is farthest from the stove, it's noticeably colder than the rest of the cabin. But that can't be helped.

After hours of unpacking, we were too exhausted to cook a proper meal, so I made a big pot of scrambled eider-duck eggs. (We bought a barrel from the crew, who gather them in their thousands and ship them back to Norway.) They're twice the size of hens' eggs, with shells of a beautiful speckled green. Delicious, although with a lingering fishy tang. I can still smell it.

I'm writing this at the main table, by the glow of a Tilley lamp. Outside it's light enough to read, but in here we need lamps, as much of the room is blind: there's only the small west window at the end, and the north one to the front.

Before we lit the stove, we could see our breath in here, but it's warmed up now. We've left the stove door open, and the red glow is cheering. I can hear rain hammering on the roof and the wind moaning in the stovepipe. Yesterday the weather turned squally. In the morning, the dogs' water pails were coated with ice. When I remarked to Eriksson that it's turning wintry, he laughed. He says that in Spitsbergen, winter doesn't begin until after Christmas.

It's eight o'clock, and we're safely inside for the night. I say "night" because although it's still light outside, it does feel like that. This evening, we saw the first faint stars.

Gus and I are at one end of the table: I'm writing this journal, and Gus is smoking and doing his notes for the expedition report. At the other end of the table, Algie has set up the Singer treadle, and is making dog harnesses. He's whistling some inane tune, and when he's not whistling, he's breathing noisily through his mouth.

So what with Algie and the treadle, it isn't exactly quiet. Added to which, there's the noise from the dogs. They're all related to each other, which is supposed to minimise fights, but you wouldn't think so to judge by what's coming from the doghouse. Growls, snarls, yelps. Scrabblings and gnawings. Bouts of oo-oo-woos. When it gets too loud, we shout and bang on the wall, and they subside into hard-done-by whines.

As usual, Mr Eriksson and the crew have gone back to the ship to sleep. It's their last night at Gruhuken, and I get the impression that they're relieved. Tomorrow we've giving a lunch in Mr Eriksson's honour. Then we'll say a fond farewell to the *Isbjørn*, and be on our own.

Later

....

I've moved to my bunk, because Algie is using his collapsible safari bath, and I'd rather not watch. All that wobbly, freckled flesh. His feet are the worst. They're flat pink slabs, and the second and third toes protrude way beyond the big toe, which I find repulsive. Gus saw me staring at them, and flushed. No doubt he's embarrassed for his "best pal".

Sometimes, though, I wonder why I'm finding it quite so hard to tolerate Algie. Maybe it's because we're so cramped in here. We're all getting hairier and dirtier, and the cabin smells of woodsmoke and unwashed clothes. You've got to duck under lines of drying socks, and pick your way between the gear. Algie's simply making it worse. He never puts anything away. And every morning he shakes out his sleeping bag and leaves it draped over the bunk "to air".

I never thought I'd say this, but I'm quite glad that we didn't get rid of the dogs. Of course I still don't *like* them, and that's not going to change, despite Gus' best efforts. Yesterday he tried to introduce me to his favourite, a scrawny russet bitch named Upik. She fawns on him, but when I approached, she growled.

I shrugged it off, but he was disappointed: with Upik, and maybe also with me. "I don't know why she did that," he said. "You're not afraid of her, I can tell."

"No," I said, "but I don't particularly like her, either. I bet she senses that."

He looked so downcast that I laughed. "Give up, Gus! You'll never make me a dog-lover."

Right now, I can hear them yowling and scratching at the wall behind my bunk. To my surprise, I don't mind the sound at all. In fact, I like it. It's reassuring to know that just behind my head, on the other side of this wall, there are living creatures. Even if they are dogs.

16th August. Midnight. First dark.

The *Isbjørn* has finally gone, and we're on our own.

My lamp casts a little pool of yellow light, and beyond it are shadows. Just now, I went to the north window. I saw the lamp's golden reflection in the panes, which are dark-blue and spangled with frost. When I cupped my hands to the glass and peered out, I saw a sprinkling of stars in an indigo sky, and the charcoal line of the bear post.

Nothing is wrong, but I want to set down what happened this afternoon. To get it straight in my mind.

Around noon, some of the crew rowed ashore, and we gave them a crate of beer as a thank-you. They've worked hard, even if it was because they're desperate to leave and get in a few weeks' sealing before the winter.

Then we had lunch with Mr Eriksson. Guessing that he'd appreciate a change from ship food, we gave him tinned ox cheek and curried vegetables with Bengal Chutney, followed by Californian pears and Singapore pineapple, then Fry's chocolate and coffee. He enjoyed it immensely, although at first he seemed intimidated by the Royal Doulton. But then Gus opened two bottles of claret and a box of cigars, and he became quite jolly. Told us how to make the trappers' speciality, blood pancakes, and gave us advice on getting through the dark time.

"Walk every day. Keep a routine. Don't *think* too much!" He added that if we ever get into "difficulty", there's a friend of his, an experienced trapper called Nils Bjørvik, overwintering on Wijdefjord, twenty miles to the west. He made quite a point about that.

Then he surprised us by producing three jars of pickled cloudberries, which he says are the best thing for warding off scurvy. (He scoffs at the notion of Vitamin C, and thinks our Redoxon tablets a waste of money.) I was touched. I think the others were, too.

After lunch, the crew still had a couple of hours' work to do, assembling our German Klepper canoes. Gus went down to the beach with Eriksson to take photographs, and Algie cleaned up the lunch things, as per our rota. To clear my head of cigar fumes, I went for a walk.

I headed upstream past the mining ruins, and at first the ground was a springy carpet of dwarf willow and moss. I walked fast, and was soon sweating. That's something I'm still getting used to, having to gauge how many layers to put on. Mr Eriksson told us a Norwegian saying: *If you're warm enough when you set out, you're wearing too many clothes.*

As I climbed higher, the going got tougher. I found myself stumbling over naked scree and brittle black lichen. The wind was sharp, and I was soon chilled. Clouds obscured the icecap, but I felt its freezing breath. When I took off my hat, my skull began to ache within seconds.

Behind the hiss of the wind and the chatter of the stream, the land lay silent. I passed the skeleton of a reindeer. I came to a standing stone by a small, cold lake. I stopped. I was aware of the noises around me — the wind, the water, my panting breath — but somehow they only deepened the stillness. I felt it as a physical presence. Immense. Overwhelming. I realised that this place is, and will always be, no-man's-land.

I suppose it's to be expected that Gruhuken should make me a little uneasy from time to time. After all, I'm town-bred, not used to the wild. But. *But.* To stand on that slope and know that there's nothing to the west of you until Greenland; nothing to the east except the Arctic Ocean; nothing to the north until the North Pole — and that's just more nothing.

With a jolt, I realised that I'd forgotten my gun. I thought of bears and started back, irked that I'd made such a basic mistake.

I'd come further than I'd intended, and below me, our camp looked like a child's toy, dwarfed by the prehistoric curves of the whale bones on the shore. Out in the bay, the *Isbjørn* was tiny. The sky was a strange, sickly yellow. The sun was sinking into the sea. In a few minutes, for the first time, it would disappear.

In the bay, an oar flashed. A rowing boat was taking a party of men back to the ship. I would have to hurry, or I'd miss saying goodbye to Eriksson.

Twilight came on as I scrambled over the stones. The wind dropped to a whisper. I heard the creak of my anorak, my labouring breath.

I was still five hundred yards above camp when I saw a man standing in front of the cabin, by the bear post. His back was turned, but I could tell it wasn't Algie or Gus. It must be one of the crew, taking a last look at the cabin he'd helped to build.

The sun was in my eyes, but I made out that he wasn't dressed like a sealer. Instead of overalls, he wore a tattered sheepskin coat and a round cap, and ragged boots.

I called out to him. "Hulloa, there! You'd better get down to the boats, or you'll be left behind!"

He turned to face me, a dark figure against the glare. Fleetingly, I saw that his hands were at his sides, and that one shoulder was higher than the other. There was something about the tilt of his head that I didn't like.

He didn't make an agreeable impression. All right, he made a *disagreeable* one. I wanted him away from my camp and safely heading for the ship. And irrationally, I wished I hadn't drawn attention to myself by calling out to him.

Feeling foolish, I continued down the slope. I had to watch my footing. When I looked again, I was relieved to see that the man had gone.

Some time later, when I reached the shore, Mr Eriksson was at the water's edge, waiting with the last of his crew to say goodbye. There was no sign of Algie or Gus, and the men seemed nervous, glancing over their shoulders at the vanishing sun.

I didn't see anyone in a sheepskin coat, so I mentioned the straggler to Mr Eriksson.

He looked at me sharply; then back to his men. Taking my arm, he drew me aside. "You make a mistake," he said in a low voice. "There was no one at the cabin."

I snorted. "Well, but there was, you know. But that's all right, he's obviously gone in the other boat."

Scowling, Eriksson shook his head. It occurred to me that he thought I might be accusing one of his men of loitering with intent to pilfer, so I said quickly, "It doesn't matter, I only mentioned it so he doesn't get left behind." I gave an awkward laugh. "After all, we'd rather not have an uninvited guest making a fourth with us in the cabin."

Eriksson didn't seem to like that. Brusquely, he asked if I'd spoken to the man. I told him no, except to urge him to hurry up and join his fellows — which, clearly, he had.

The Norwegian opened his mouth to reply, but just then Gus and Algie came running down, bearing our parting gift of claret and cigars, so he lost his chance. Algie and Gus made embarrassed little speeches of thanks, and Eriksson reddened and thanked them back. His manner was strained. I don't think they noticed.

When it was my turn, he took my hand and crushed it in his bear's grip. "Good winter, Professor," he said, his grey eyes holding mine. At the time, I couldn't make out his expression. But now I wonder if it wasn't pity.

Then he was in the boat, and his men were pushing off. As it rocked over the waves, he glanced back — not at us, but behind us to the cabin. I couldn't help doing the same. All I saw were the dogs, yowling and straining at their stakes.

The three of us stood and watched the boat reach the *Isbjørn*. We watched the men climb on board. We watched them raise the boat. We heard the sputter of the engine as the ship gathered speed. By now, all that remained of the sun was a crimson slash on the horizon.

Suddenly, Algie clapped his hand to his forehead, then turned and raced up the beach. When he reached the bear post, he hoisted the "flag" he'd almost forgotten: a dead fulmar which he'd shot that morning. He strung it up by one wing, and the wind caught it and made it flap, a parody of flight. Out in the bay, the *Isbjørn* dipped her ensign in reply.

As the sun's dying glimmer turned the sea to bronze, we watched the ship disappear behind the headland.

"And then there were three," said Algie.

Gus made no reply. I repressed a movement of irritation.

"Stay there," Algie commanded. Running back to the cabin again, he swiftly returned with his camping canteen: two crystal bottles of whisky and water, with three nested nickel tumblers in a leather carrying case. He also bore a mysterious, sacking-wrapped parcel; this turned out to be a lump of ice which he'd hacked from the icecap the day before.

"For the first time in weeks," he panted, "the sun is *officially* over the yardarm."

He was right. The sun was gone. Banks of grey cloud were rolling in, obliterating its dying glow.

I turned back to the others, and we drank a welcome to the night.

CHAPTER
SEVEN

I think I was a little on edge before, but I'm not any more. A couple of weeks' hard routine work has set me right.

Up at six thirty, pulling on your clothes before the stove. The man on dog duty lets them out; the man on kitchen duty starts the coffee. Reading duty means trudging out to the Stevenson screen (which is like a beehive on legs, with a louvred screen to protect the self-registering instruments inside). At seven o'clock you read the charts, then check the anemometer, wind vane, snowfall and hoar frost (on a little brass sphere like an alchemist's globe).

At seven thirty I'm on the bicycle generator, wiring the readings to the Government Station on Bear Island, from where they go to the forecasting system in England. Breakfast's at eight: bread baked by "Mrs Balfour", with bacon and eggs or porridge. At noon there's a second set of readings and transmissions, and another at five. The dogs are fed at six. In between it's hunting and collecting driftwood; Algie's off on his geological survey (to my relief), and I go in the boat with Gus and help him net plankton and little swimming snails.

Once a week I coax the Austin to life, and we contact England with messages for family and friends, and dispatches to *The Times* and our sponsors. Gus writes these: chatty pieces about the wildlife and the dogs. England feels more and more remote, and he's finding it harder to think what to say.

The weather changes so fast it's bewildering. Two weeks ago, frost turned the dwarf willows on the slopes scarlet, like splashes of blood. Ten days later, we left the bunkroom window open a crack, and woke to an invasion of fog. Last night we had our first snowfall. Like schoolboys we stood with our faces upturned to the fast-falling flakes. Now Gruhuken is clothed in white. Even the doghouse has become a structure of purity and grace. The snow has changed the feel of the camp. Snow hushes everything but footfalls. That takes some getting used to.

The nights are growing longer with alarming speed: twenty minutes more each day.

What do I mean, alarming? I like it. By now I'm used to living cheek by jowl with the others, and I enjoy the long evenings in the cabin. Gus working at his microscope, calling me over to peer at some fresh marvel, then chaffing me when I pretend not to understand. Algie cleaning guns and labelling fossils. (He remains an annoyance, but Gus has vetoed the baths, on the grounds that they make too much mess; and as it turns colder, not even Algie is assiduous about sponge baths.) We smoke and listen to the wireless. And I catch up on the latest wild theories in physics. Before I left London, my old professor sent me a stack of periodicals. As I read them, I feel a flicker of excitement. I remember how I used to feel. How I used to dream.

I think about that when I work at my wireless bench. Sometimes I catch sight of my reflection in the window. I hardly know myself. My hair is longer, and my beard makes me look younger, more hopeful. I feel hopeful. Maybe Gus has a point. Maybe I haven't missed my chance.

It's odd, but the wireless corner is so cold that I have to put on an extra pullover. And at times there's a faint, disagreeable smell of seaweed. I've washed everything with Lysol, but it's still there. I don't think the others have noticed.

But I do still love Gruhuken. It's a million miles away from the shabby gentility of Tooting; from worrying about whether your collar can go another day. My poor mother lived for all that. I remember her "doing the steps" at our house in Bexhill. She had a girl to do the rough, but the steps were her domain. She did the ones at the door with white hearthstone, those by the gate with grey. Thinking of that now, it's heartbreaking. To spend your life painting stones.

Gus loves it here too, because there aren't any servants; he says this is the first time he's ever been allowed to make his own bed. I'm not sure about Algie. He insists on having the wireless or the gramophone on all the time, and now he's taken to whistling through his teeth. Sometimes I think he can't bear a moment's silence. What's he trying to escape?

Over the last few days, great flocks of birds have begun to gather in the bay. Gus says they're getting ready to leave.

30th August
···

Gus was right, the dogs did get me in the end. Well, one of them did.

Until this afternoon, I'd only progressed as far as learning their names. The leaders of the pack are Upik the russet bitch, and her mate Svarten. Eli, Kiawak, Pakomi and Jens are their progeny; and Isaak and Anadark are the youngsters, only a year old, although they look like full-grown wolves. Isaak's the one who fell in the harbour at Tromsø.

Yesterday, Gus and Algie were off hunting and I was reading in the cabin when all hell broke loose outside. Thinking instantly of bears, I pulled on my gear, grabbed my rifle and burst out the door.

Thank God, no bears. The dogs were baying and straining at their stakes to get at the youngster, Isaak. Somehow he'd found a tin of pemmican, gnawed his way through, and got his muzzle stuck inside. He was stumbling blindly about, clunking his helmeted head against rocks.

When he heard me coming, he stopped. I didn't give myself time to think, I just ran over and clamped my knees about his middle, the way Gus and Algie do when they're putting on harnesses. Isaak squirmed, but couldn't get free, and I yanked the tin off his head.

God, he was fast. Leapt up and gave me a headbutt that knocked me flat and sent the tin flying. He pounced on it — and got his head stuck *again*.

"Bad dog! Bad dog!" I shouted inanely as I struggled to my feet. Then we went through it all again — only this time when I got the tin off his head, I jumped out of the way. I was so pleased with myself that I emptied the pemmican in the snow for him, and he downed it in one gulp, then stood lashing his tail, his ice-blue eyes alight with anarchy. *Let's do it again!*

Damn, damn, damn. He'd torn one ear on the tin. After what he'd just put me through, I wasn't going to let him get lockjaw, so I unclipped him from his stake and dragged him towards the cabin for treatment. Halfway there, I realised I should've fetched the disinfectant first, leaving him tied up outside. He seemed to think so too, as he gave me a doubtful look.

The trick to handling a husky is to grab it by its harness and half lift it, so that its front paws don't touch the ground; this way, it can't run off with you. At least that's the theory; I'd never tried it till now. Half lifting Isaak in what I hoped was the approved manner, I hauled him through the front door, grabbed a bottle of disinfectant from the shelf in the hall, and hauled him out again. By the time I'd got him safely tied to his stake, I was sweating. Huskies aren't huge, but by God, they're strong.

Muttering, "Good boy, there's a good husky," I sloshed on the disinfectant. He didn't even growl. I think he was too surprised. When it was over, I was so relieved that I gave him another tin of pemmican as a reward.

Gus and Algie came back and I told them what had happened. Algie huffed and said I oughtn't to favour one dog in front of the others. Gus just grinned. I said there's nothing to grin about, that's the stupidest dog I've ever seen, imagine getting your head stuck in a tin *twice*.

Gus burst out laughing. "Stupid? Jack, he got two tins of pemmican out of you!"

Since then, Isaak's been on the lookout for me. If I happen to glance his way, he lashes his tail and makes croaky ror-ror-ror noises. And this afternoon when I was smoking a cigarette, he came and leaned against my leg.

15th September

The birds are leaving and the nights are getting longer.

It's dark when we wake up and dark when we eat supper. When I'm out on the boardwalk looking in, the windows glow a welcoming orange, and the main room is lit up like a theatre. But when I'm at the Stevenson screen, the mountains loom, and I get the sense of the dark waiting to reclaim the land. Then I'm keen to get back inside and draw the curtains and shut out the night. Only I can't, as we haven't got any.

In one of my periodicals, there's a paper by someone who's worked out that what we know of the universe is only a tiny percentage of what actually exists. He says what's left can't be seen or detected, but it's there; he calls it "dark matter". Of course, no one believes him; but I find the idea unsettling. Or rather, not the idea itself, that's merely an odd notion about outer space. What I don't like is the feeling I sometimes get that other things might exist around us, of which we know nothing.

In a month, on the 16th of October, we'll see the sun for the last time. According to the books, there'll still be *some* light for a few weeks after that, because at noon, the sun won't be all that far below the horizon. They call it the "midday dawn". After that, nothing.

But my God, the colours we're seeing now! If it's clear, dawn turns the sky an amazing pinkish gold. The snow glitters like diamonds. The whale ribs on the shore are dazzling. The roof of the cabin is blanketed in white, its walls crusted with frost. After a few hours, the light turns, and the bay becomes a sheet of bronze. The day dies in a blaze of astonishing colour: crimson, magenta, violet.

So much light.

And now this.

It was after supper, and I was reading and smoking at the table. Algie was playing patience and drumming a tattoo with his fingers, and Gus was outside checking on the dogs. Suddenly he burst in. "Chaps! Outside, quick!"

As it was minus ten, "quick" meant a feverish dragging on of boots, jumpers, waterproofs, mufflers, mittens and hats.

It was worth it.

"The dogs' fur was crackling with static," murmured Gus. "That's how I knew."

We stood craning our necks at the Northern Lights. Photographs don't do them justice. It's the movement which impresses you most. The way those luminous pale-green waves roll and break and ripple across the sky — and vanish, and appear again somewhere else — and all in eerie silence. A sea of light. I know that for some people they're a religious experience, but I found them intimidating. Those great, shimmering waves . . . so vast, so distant. Utterly indifferent to what lies beneath. And in a strange way, that extraordinary light seems only to emphasise the darkness beyond.

Algie broke the spell by whistling, and for once I didn't mind. Soon afterwards, he went inside.

The two of us stayed, watching the sky.

Gus said quietly, "Hard not to be moved, isn't it?"

I grunted.

With his heel, he hacked at the snow. "I read somewhere that the Eskimos believe they're the torches of the dead, lighting the way for the living." He hesitated. "They say that if you whistle, the souls of the dead will draw nearer."

I threw him a sharp glance, but he was staring at his boots.

"D'you believe in any of that, Jack?" His face was grave. In the lamplight, frost glinted in his beard.

"Believe in what?" I said guardedly. "Spirits brandishing torches?"

"No, no of course not. I mean . . . unseen forces. That sort of thing." Embarrassed, he hacked again at the snow.

I guessed what he meant by "that sort of thing", but I didn't want to talk about it, not in the dark, so I pretended I didn't understand. "I believe in the wind," I said. "That's an unseen force. And radio waves."

For a moment he was silent. Then he snorted a laugh. "Very well, then. Be the literal-minded scientist."

"I'm not," I replied. To prove it, I told him what I'd been reading in the professor's periodicals.

I must have waxed enthusiastic, because his lip curled. "And you envy them, don't you, Jack?"

"What?"

"Those physicists in their laboratories. You want to be the one thinking up the crazy theories about the universe."

It was my turn to be embarrassed. And flattered, that he should know me so well. Because he's right, I am jealous. That *should* be me, dreaming up mad ideas in a physics lab.

And maybe I could do it, after all. Maybe when we get back to England, I can find some way of going in for a further degree. Gus thinks I can. That's got to count for something.

So now as I sit here writing, I keep breaking off to fantasise about the insights I'll gain at Gruhuken, and how I'll astonish the world on my return:

How things change! When we first got here, my nerves were on edge. All that brooding about "the great stillness", and getting spooked by some sealer in a sheepskin coat. But now that Gruhuken is really ours, I'm not on edge any more.

1st October
....

I can't stand it, he's insufferable. I know the dogs need fresh meat, and I know that means shooting a few seals. But Jesus Christ.

Yesterday I went with him in the canoe, and I got lucky and shot a seal. We rowed like hell and gaffed it before it sank, then dragged it back to shore. The dogs were going frantic at their stakes. Gus ran down to help cut up the carcass.

Algie was chief butcher, because of course he's the expert after six weeks in Greenland. So there he is, skinning it — or should I say "flensing" it — with his nasty great "flensing knife" (why can't he just call it a knife?). But as he's slitting the belly, the creature shudders. Its guts are spilling out, its blood soaking the snow, that hot-copper smell catching at my throat, but its eyes are big and soft as plums — *alive*.

"Christ, it's not dead!" I croak as I scrabble for a rock to finish it off. Gus has gone white and he's fumbling for his knife. Algie calmly goes on skinning. It's only when he reaches the bit over the heart that he sticks in his knife and ends it.

Why? To show us how tough he is? Or is it because he hates this place, and he's getting his own back?

I told him he made me sick. He said if I felt like that I should've done something, not just watched. We

80

would have come to blows if Gus hadn't hauled me away, leaving Algie fuming.

"I know he's been your friend for ever," I told Gus when I'd got myself under control, "although why that should be I cannot begin to fathom. But you saw what he did. Tell me you're not going to make excuses for him."

Gus flushed. "No excuses. Not this time."

I was fiercely glad about that.

You'd think skinning a seal alive would be enough, but today Algie went further — or he would have done, if the two of us hadn't stopped him.

For days he's been trying to prevent the dogs from chewing their harnesses, and this afternoon he declared that enough's enough, and grabbed his geological hammer.

"What the hell are you doing with that?" I said.

"Don't worry, old man," he said breezily. "It's just an Eskimo trick I know. You break their back teeth. Works a treat."

Gus and I stared at him, appalled.

Algie rolled his eyes as if we were imbeciles. "It's practically painless! You simply hang them up till they pass out, then tap away with the hammer. They're a tad woozy for a while, but they soon pick up. Huskies are tough as steel, don't you know?"

Slowly, I rose to my feet. "If you go near those dogs with that hammer, I'll smash your face in."

"Jack." Gus put a hand on my shoulder.

I shook him off. "I mean it, Algie."

"I don't care if you do, old man," said Algie, turning pink. "You're not in charge of the dogs. I am."

"I'm not an old man," I said, "and I'm more than capable of stopping you, so —"

"Jack, no," said Gus. "Leave this to me." He turned to Algie. His eyes were glassy, his features chiselled in marble. "As leader of this expedition, I am telling you, Algie, that I absolutely forbid this. Do I make myself clear?"

Algie's pale eyelashes quivered. Then he heaved a sigh and flung down his hammer. "Lord, what a rumpus over a few dogs!"

I don't think he has the faintest conception of what the "rumpus" was about. I think he genuinely believes that animals don't feel pain. And of course, I'm a Nancy boy for believing that they do.

If he touches Isaak, I'll break *his* teeth. See how he likes it.

6th October
....

We're down to a few hours' daylight.

Dawn comes, and deep down, you can't help believing that there's a full day ahead. It's a shock when you realise that the light's already on the turn, and soon it'll be night again. It's hard to get used to, that sense of the dark gaining ascendancy. Waiting to take over.

At the moment there's a moon, so it isn't too bad, but you know that it won't last long. Strange. In the summer, when it was light all the time, the moon was so faint you hardly noticed it. Now you follow its every move.

I'm trying to train myself to find my way in the dark without a torch. I don't like the way the beam of light draws your eye and renders what's beyond impenetrable. I suppose it's the same as when you're inside the cabin and you light a lamp and it prevents you seeing outside. Or rather, it doesn't completely prevent it; there's a gradation. Light one lamp, and you can still make out the dogs, or the bear post. With two lamps, it's harder. With three, all you see is the lamps' own reflections in the panes. A commonplace observation, of course, but here it strikes me afresh. How odd, that light should prevent one from seeing.

It's colder, minus fifteen today. Stoking the stove is becoming a preoccupation. And it takes an age to get dressed, even if it's only to fetch logs from the woodpile, right outside the door. When you come back, you've got to brush the snow off your clothes and pick frost out of your beard before entering the cabin. Last week we had to break the ice on the stream to reach the water. Now there is no water, and it's a bucket of ice that we bring back to the cabin.

The birds have gone. The cliffs are silent. There's a sense of something waiting.

12th October

Four days before the sun goes for good.

Dawn comes, then turns to dusk, with nothing in between. But for the past three days we haven't even seen that, because of the fog. Camp is an island, floating in grey. No colours, just grey. And the stillness.

You feel this constant anxiety. It's childish but real; you worry that you're going to miss the last of the sun. Every day you wake up and tell yourself *surely* the fog's lifted? But it hasn't. And by lunchtime you know that you're facing another twenty-four hours of this dead grey stillness. What if the fog doesn't lift until it's too late?

That's probably why I'm not sleeping too well. I know I have dreams, and that they're dark and exhausting, because I wake up unrested, with a sense of a struggle. But I can't remember.

It's not just me. Algie gets up during the night, and Gus moans in his sleep. And sometimes I come inside and they're talking, but they fall silent when they see me. I shouldn't mind, but I do. It hurts. I thought that business with the seal had opened Gus' eyes. Surely he can't be drifting back to Algie? The dogs are unsettled, too. And when we let them off for a run, they always head for the eastern end of the bay, never the west.

Today it was my turn for the five o'clock readings. Dark, of course, but even in fog, the snow creates a kind of dim grey gloom. You can find your way if you know the terrain, and although you can't make out faces, you can recognise creatures by how they move: an Arctic fox, a dog, a man.

My breath crackled in my nostrils as I trudged to the Stevenson screen. I had to watch my footing. Five days ago it rained, and there's ice under the snow, which makes it treacherous.

I don't like the way you bring your noise with you. I don't like it that your hood cuts off your vision, so you don't know what's behind you.

Last week I tried bringing Isaak with me, on a rope clipped to his harness. It didn't work. He was nervous, panting and setting back his ears. I think it's because the Stevenson screen is only about thirty yards from the rocks, and for some reason he doesn't like them. Maybe it's just that he's scared of the sea.

We're all a little on edge. It'll be better once the sun's gone for good, and we can forget about it and get on with things.

16th October

I've seen it.

Writing the words makes me break out in a cold sweat. But I have to set it down. I have to make sense of it.

The sky cleared just before noon, so we got our last sight of the sun after all. It was Gus' turn to take the readings at the Stevenson screen, but I went with him to watch the sun rise and set — which by now is pretty much the same thing. Algie stayed inside. He said it would spook him to see it go. This time, no one suggested a ceremonial whisky.

Twilight. Behind the bird cliffs, the red glow of dawn, but to the west it was night: the cold glimmer of stars. The black bones of the mountains jutted through the snow. On the shore, the whale ribs glinted with frost, and the rocks sloping down to the sea were white and smooth. The water was dark purple, vivid and strange.

Because of the cliffs, we couldn't see much. We saw the sky turn bloody and inflamed as the sun struggled to rise. We saw a sliver of fire. An abortive dawn. The sun sank back, defeated.

Gone.

I shut my eyes and it was still there, blazing behind my eyelids. I opened them. Gone. All that remained was a crimson glow.

"So that's that," Gus said quietly.

Four months without the sun. It doesn't seem real.

In the doghouse, the dogs began to howl.

"They feel it too," said Gus.

I forced a smile. "Gus, I think they're just hungry."

His mouth twisted. "Well, they'll have to wait a few hours. Are you coming in?"

"In a bit." I still had time before I was due to transmit the readings. I didn't want to lose any of that crimson glow.

Listening to the diminishing crunch of Gus' boots, I watched it fade behind the cliffs, like embers growing cold. The moon wasn't yet up, but there was still enough light to see by. No wind. The dogs had stopped howling.

Out of nowhere, for no reason, I was afraid. Not merely apprehensive. This was deep, visceral, pounding dread. My skin prickled. My heart thudded in my throat. My senses were stretched taut. My body knew before I did that I was not alone.

86

Thirty yards away on the rocks, something moved.

I tried to cry out. My tongue stuck to the roof of my mouth.

It crouched at the edge of the rocks. It was streaming wet. It had just hauled itself from the sea. And yet the stillness was absolute. No sound of droplets pattering on snow. No creak of waterproofs as it rose. Slowly. Awkwardly.

It stood. It faced me. Dark, dark against the sea. I saw its arms hanging at its sides. I saw that one shoulder was higher than the other. I saw its wet round head.

I knew at once that it wasn't some trapper from a nearby camp, or a polar mirage, or that hoary excuse, "a trick of the light". The mind does not suggest explanations which don't fit the facts, only to reject them a moment later. I knew what it was. I *knew*, with some ancient part of me, that it wasn't alive.

Behind me the cabin door creaked open. Yellow light spilled on to the snow.

"Jack?" called Gus. "It's nearly twelve thirty. The transmission . . ."

I tried to reply. I couldn't.

The rocks were empty. It was gone.

I stood breathing through my mouth. I stammered an answer to Gus; I said I was fine, told him I was coming in soon.

He shut the door and the light blinked out.

I've never felt such reluctance as I felt then, but I made myself — I *willed* myself — to take my electric

87

torch from my pocket and walk down the beach and on to those rocks.

The snow crust was brittle as glass beneath my boots. Pristine. No tracks. No marks of a man hauling himself out of the sea. I'd known that there wouldn't be. But I'd needed to see for myself.

I stood with my hands at my sides, hearing the slap of waves and the clink of ice.

The dread had drained away, leaving bewilderment. My thoughts whirled. It can't be. But I saw it. It can't be. But I did see it.

And I know, although I can't say *how* I know, that what I saw on those rocks was the same figure I saw at the bear post, two months ago at first dark.

It's real. I saw it.

It isn't alive.

CHAPTER
EIGHT

17th October
....

All day I've been trying to get it straight in my mind. What did I see? Should I tell the others?

When I got back to the cabin, it was 12.29, and I had to scramble to do the transmissions. I was two people. One was a wireless operator pedalling the bicycle generator; clipboard in his left hand, tapping the key with his right. The other was a man who'd just seen a ghost rise out of the sea.

I can't remember what I did after that. But I remember looking around me at the cabin. The orange glow of lamplight, the socks and dishcloths on the line above the stove. Gus and Algie tucking into Paterson's Oat Cakes and Golden Syrup. I didn't feel part of it. They were on one side, I was on the other. I thought, how can all this exist in the same world as *that?*

Somehow, I got through the rest of the day. And oddly enough, I slept like a log.

It was Algie's turn to do the readings today, thank God. I was on kitchen duty. I clung to it the way they say a drowning man clings to straws.

For breakfast I made what Algie calls "boarding-house kedgeree". I told myself, *this* is reality. The smell of coffee. The buttery taste of salt cod and hard-boiled egg.

I didn't set foot outside the cabin, except to go to the outhouse. I scrubbed the kitchen and washed clothes. Made cheese scones and seal meat hash for lunch. Tried to read one of the professor's periodicals. Saw to the transmissions.

For dinner I made my pemmican stew. Pemmican is a mix of lean and fat beef, dried and compressed into blocks with albumen. You break it into lumps and boil it with water. Too much water and you've got a slimy sludge; too little and it's disgusting. I usually get it about right. I add potatoes, dried vegetables, and my secret ingredient — Oxo — for a salty, filling stew.

Concealment is hard work. I was almost too exhausted to eat. Algie, too, seemed tired, and Gus was out of sorts and picked at his food. None of us suggested the wireless, and we turned in early.

I'm writing this in my bunk. Behind my head, scuffles are coming from the doghouse. Tomorrow it's my turn to do the readings. I'm dreading it. I'm going to take Isaak.

I can't face telling the others, not yet. I wish I could believe that what I saw on the rocks was all in my mind, because then it wouldn't be real. But I know that's not true. I felt that dread. I saw what I saw.

Gruhuken is haunted.

There. I've said it. That's why Eriksson didn't want to bring us here. That's why the crew always slept on the ship, and were so anxious to leave before first dark.

But what does it mean, "haunted"?

I looked it up in Gus' dictionary. *To haunt: 1. To visit (a person or place) in the form of a ghost. 2. To recur (memory, thoughts, etc.), e.g. he was haunted by the fear of insanity. 3. To visit frequently. [From ON heimta, to bring home, OE hamettan, to give a home to.]*

I wish I hadn't read that. To think that something so horrible should have its roots in something so — well, homely.

But what *is* it?

It's an echo, that's what it is. An echo from the past. I've read about that; it's called "place memory", a well-known idea, been around since the Victorians. If something happens in a place — something intensely emotional or violent — it imprints itself on that place; maybe by altering the atmosphere, like radio waves, or by affecting matter, so that rocks, for example, become in some way charged with what occurred. Then if a receptive person comes along, the place plays back the event, or snatches of it. You simply need to be there to pick it up. And who better to do that than a wireless operator? Ha ha ha.

Yes, this has to be it. I don't think I'm clutching at straws. What else could it be? It's the only explanation that makes any sense.

And it means, too, that what I saw on the rocks doesn't actually exist. It did once, but it doesn't now. That's what I've got to hold on to.

What I saw was only an echo.

But an echo of what?

It's five in the morning and I've got to sort this out before I do the seven o'clock reading.

An echo of what?

It has to be something that happened here. Something bad. I know it was bad, because of the dread.

I've flicked through my books on Spitsbergen, but I didn't find any mention of Gruhuken. And I've been over this journal and reread what I wrote about the men who were here before us. There isn't much, and I'm not sure how accurate it is, because at the time, I wasn't interested. I didn't think it was important. First there were trappers, then miners, that's what Eriksson said. All those bones, and the mining ruins, and that tangle of wire on the beach. The claim signs. The hut.

That hut. The desolation when I crawled inside. Did some trapper or miner do away with himself in there? Is that what this is about?

I need to know. It's a compulsion, a dreadful curiosity. The same curiosity, I suppose, which made me stop on the Embankment that night, and watch them pull that body from the Thames.

Time to get dressed and see to those bloody readings. I'm definitely taking Isaak.

Should I tell the others what I saw?

Three days since I saw it, and nothing. No problems yesterday doing the readings. Isaak wasn't the slightest bit uneasy. He tried to dig a hole under the Stevenson screen.

That gave me courage, so I took him with me to look over the beach and the mining ruins for clues. Of course I didn't find anything. Not in the dark, with everything covered in snow. And to be honest, I couldn't bring myself to stay out there for long. To make myself feel less of a coward, I went to the bear post and cut down Algie's "flag": that dead fulmar which has been dangling there for weeks. I thought it would have rotted, but of course it's been too cold. Isaak demolished it in minutes.

Three days without incident, and I'm feeling a little better. *Nothing in life is to be feared. It is only to be understood.* She was right, old Marie Curie. I was frightened because I didn't understand what I saw. Now that I do — or at least have a working hypothesis — I can deal with it.

I'll probably have to tell the others at some point, but not yet. Talking about it would make it real.

That makes me think of Mother. She was a great one for not talking about things. She always refused to discuss what was wrong with Father. She used to say, no, Jack, it'll only make it real. That used to infuriate me. I'd say, but it *is* real. And she'd say, well, more real, then. And she was right.

This afternoon, out of the blue, Algie asked if I wanted to come dog-sledging, and suddenly I did, very much. It's exactly what I need: hard physical work. To hell with everything else. I've been feeling a bit sorry for Algie. He's not a complete fool, he knows he's been getting on our nerves, and he knows that Gus prefers me. And I think he feels bad about that business with the seal, and the dogs' teeth. Maybe asking me to go sledging was his way of building bridges.

The sledge was behind the outhouse, where it had frozen fast, so we had to hack it free. Then we had to harness the dogs and clip them to their traces. They knew at once what was up, and went wild, because they *love* to run. And Isaak must have told the others that I'm OK, because they were actually quite well behaved with me.

The sledge is hardwood with steel-shod runners, and virtually indestructible: it runs on snow, ice, even naked rock. Algie and I stood on the back, and as soon as he unhooked the brake, we were off: the dogs running silently and in earnest, in Eskimo fantail formation, which looks chaotic compared to the European two-by-two, but turns out to be strangely effective.

God, it was exhilarating. We jolted and shook so violently that I was nearly flung clear. Didn't bother with headlamps; you see more without them, as your eyes adjust to starlight and snow glow. We rattled west, over the thick pebbly ice of the stream, then past the rocks. No time to be scared. Not with the patter of paws and the scrape of the sledge, the dogs' tails curling to right or left; and now and then the sharp

94

smell as one of them defecated. It was fast and intense, vividly alive.

Algie doesn't use a whip, he just calls *ille-ille* for right, or *yuk-yuk* for left, and they turn. We ran south over snow-covered shingle, along the edge of the Wijdefjord. Isaak, at the far right of the fantail, kept glancing round at me. Once, he decided he'd had enough, and doubled back and jumped on to the sledge. I couldn't help laughing as I shoved him off. "No hitching a lift, you lazy brute!"

Algie halted to rest the team, turning the sledge on its side so they couldn't run off with it. Upik and Svarten, the most experienced, lay down sedately and cooled their bellies, while the others rolled in the snow or chewed it, or stood panting, their long tongues lolling.

Algie went to help Jens and Anadark, who'd got tangled up, and I ambled over to say hello to Isaak. His back was sprinkled with snow, but his fur is so thick that it didn't melt. Nosing my thigh, he leaned against me. No jumping up, he's not that sort of dog.

To the south, the fjord thrust deep into the mountains. Somewhere on the other side was the hut of that trapper friend of Eriksson's, but I couldn't see any lights. The mountains were deep charcoal, streaked with grey snow. The sea was black.

I thought of the way home, past the rocks, and shivered.

Until then, I'd assumed that if I told anyone, it would be Gus. But now, as I watched Algie bending over the dogs, I had a sudden urge to blurt it out to him. *The oddest thing happened to me the other day on the rocks . . .*

My next thought was, what if he thinks I'm losing my nerve? He'll tell Gus. What if they start to wonder whether they can rely on me?

Or what if — what if I tell Algie and he looks at me and says, I'm glad you saw it, Jack, because I've seen it too.

So I didn't tell Algie. And I didn't tell Gus when we got back to the cabin. And now, as I write this in my bunk before turning in, I regret that. I'm sick of bearing this on my own. I can't do it any more.

First thing tomorrow. Breakfast. I'll tell them at breakfast.

22nd October
....

Too late. You lost your chance. They're gone.

Gus didn't get up for breakfast. He lay in his bunk, feverish and pale. I was annoyed. I wanted — no, I *needed* — him to be better. I didn't believe he could be genuinely ill.

Not even when the fever got worse and he lay with one knee drawn up, clutching his belly. The Red Cross first-aid manual was no help. Nor were Andrews Liver Salts. I wired Longyearbyen, and had a laborious question-and-answer session with the doctor in Morse. He said it sounded like appendicitis and he was on his way.

I don't remember much of the last two days. Algie and I did what we could for Gus with hot-water bottles and morphine. We fed ourselves and the dogs, and kept up the readings and transmissions. None of us talked much. We were all thinking, what happens now? Is this the end?

The doctor arrived in the *Isbjørn* — it had been at the settlement when we'd wired for help — and after that, things happened fast.

Strange to see other people when it's been just the three of us for nearly two months. But there was no time to take it in. The doctor said he didn't need to operate here (thank God), but Gus had to come back to Longyearbyen and have the appendix out there. And one of us must go with him, "in case anything happened".

For one wild moment, I was desperate for it to be me. Leave this place, get the hell out of here. Gus needs you.

Gus needs you. That's what changed my mind. He cares about the expedition as deeply as I do. And if I went and Algie stayed, that would be the end. Algie would never have the discipline to go it alone. And Gus would know that I could've done it, I could've saved the expedition, but I funked it.

All this flashed through my mind as I hauled Algie over to the wireless corner, leaving the doctor and Mr Eriksson in the bunkroom with Gus.

"You go," I told him.

He glanced at me and then away. "What about you?"

"I'll have to stay, won't I?" I snapped.

"But — surely not on your own."

"Well what the fuck do you suggest?"

He swallowed. "You could come too. The doctor says if all goes well, it'll only be a few weeks, then we can come back and carry on."

"The dogs, Algie! What about the fucking dogs? No time to take them with us, is there? And we can't just leave them! We *could* try paying a couple of Eriksson's men to stay and look after them, but somehow I don't think they'd say yes. So where does that leave us? Hm? Eriksson would tell us to shoot the brutes and have done with it, but I couldn't do that. Could you?"

He gave me an odd look. "You're so rational, Jack."

"*Rational?*" I kneaded my forehead. "Listen. Even if I came, d'you think that's what Gus wants? The whole expedition shot to hell because I can't hold the fort for a couple of weeks?"

He didn't argue. I think he'd only objected as a sop to his conscience. And he never once offered to change places.

They got Gus on to the stretcher, and Algie crammed a few things in a rucksack, then we made our way down to the shore. A squally night, sleet falling fast in the lamplight. As they manoeuvred the stretcher into the boat, Eriksson seized me by the arm and pulled me aside. He said I couldn't stay here alone, I had to go with them. We argued it out in the bitter snow. I won. But then he peered into my face and said, "This is a bad mistake. The one who walks. You have seen it. *Ja?*"

Now that shook me. Maybe, deep down, I'd been hoping all along that it *was* only in my mind; and here was Georg Eriksson, hard-bitten skipper of the *Isbjørn*, finally putting paid to that idea.

"It doesn't matter what I saw," I told him. "I can't leave the dogs, and I can't scupper the expedition because of an echo!"

He didn't understand what I meant by that, but before I could explain, they were calling him: the boat was ready to leave. And I was running over to say goodbye to Gus.

That's when it hit me. Gus is really ill. Gus could die.

I felt as if I'd been kicked in the stomach. Gus could die.

He lay bundled up on the stretcher. In the lamplight, his face looked carved in stone, disturbingly like an effigy.

"Jack," he panted. "Are you sure about this? You can still change your mind and come with us."

"No I can't," I said as gently as I could. "I can't let the expedition go to blazes. Besides. Couple of weeks and you'll be back again, right as rain."

"Thanks, Jack. Thanks most frightfully." Slipping off his mitten, he moved his hand.

I gripped it hard. "I'll miss you."

He forced a grin. "Me too. Be careful, Jack. Be *careful*. Keep the dogs with you."

"Don't you worry, I'll look after them. Don't worry. Just get better."

He licked his lips. "Good show, Jack. I can't tell you . . ." He sucked in his breath. "Good show."

And it *was* a good show I put on, a bloody good show, as I stood in the shallows watching the boat make its way between the icebergs; as I listened to the putter of the engine, and saw the lights of the *Isbjørn* heading west. Jack Miller, saviour of the expedition. Heroically holding the fort till the others return. The lights blinked out. Quite suddenly, I was alone, with the grey sea sucking at my boots, in this night that has no end.

But what the hell was I supposed to do? How could I let the whole thing founder because of a few damned echoes from the past? I can just see myself explaining that to the Royal Geographical Society. "Frightfully sorry, chaps, couldn't carry on. Saw a ghost."

How could I do that to Gus?

Besides, I'm not alone here, not really. I've got the dogs. And the wireless. And there's that trapper in Wijdefjord if I ever need help.

I'm protesting too much, I know that.

But the thing to remember, Jack, is that it's only an echo. It's like a footprint or a shadow. It can't hurt you. All it can do is frighten.

CHAPTER
NINE

Well I got through the first day.

Routine, that's the ticket. Readings at seven, noon and five o'clock; transmissions half an hour after. I've had the dogs with me, and so far, no problems — except catching them again. A handful of sweets works wonders: brandy balls and Fruitines. I save the butterscotch for Isaak.

As I bustle about, cooking, wirelessing, chopping wood, feeding and watering the dogs, I feel oddly self-conscious. "Now then," I say out loud, "what's for breakfast? Fried eggs? And what about dinner? All right then, curry it is!"

And I notice that I address myself as "we". Not "I" or "you" or "Jack". I don't like to acknowledge my solitude out loud.

There's a novelty to spreading my things around the cabin and eating what I like. For supper last night I invented a hearty dish of onions and tinned steak pudding fried with potatoes and cheese. I keep the stove well stoked, the lamps trimmed and the water barrel full, using the rough-and-ready system we devised: top up barrel with snow, pour on boiling water from kettle; refill kettle with more snow, place on stove to melt. Whatever I do, I do without a pause. I don't like the silence when I stop.

The worst thing about being alone is that when I go out to the Stevenson screen or for my walk with the dogs, I can't leave the stove lit or a single lamp burning in the cabin, in case of fire. That's an even more vital rule than the one about closing doors. It means I return to a cold, still, dark cabin. I try not to look at the blind black windows as I approach. When I'm in the porch, my steps sound too loud, my breath like that of someone else. I hate the moment when I close the door behind me and I'm shut in the long, dark hall. In the beam of my torch, everyday things leap from the shadows. The waterproofs on the hooks look like — well, not like empty clothes.

The main room is freezing. It smells of woodsmoke and paraffin. And it's so still.

There's a sliver of moon but soon there'll be none. I'm going to hang a storm lantern from the antlers over the porch.

Last night I tried the gramophone, then the wireless, but the disembodied voices made me feel more isolated. So instead I sat and read, with the hiss of the lamps and the crackle of the stove, and the tick of Gus' travelling alarm clock. It's olive-green calfskin, smooth and cool to the touch, and its gold-rimmed face is beautifully plain. I keep it near me.

I miss Gus more than I've ever missed anyone. Strange, that. I was ten when Father died, and although I loved him, I soon stopped missing him; perhaps because he'd been ill for years, and I'd done my grieving when he was alive. Same with Mother. She was worn out, she wanted to go. So I didn't miss either of them for long. Nothing like this. This savage ache that came on as soon as he left.

Is this what it's like to have a brother? Or a best friend? It's confusing. I don't quite know what I mean. And I hate Algie for being with him when I'm not.

It's eight in the evening as I write this, sitting at the table with a whisky, and three lamps brightly ablaze. To anyone standing on the boardwalk looking in, I'd be clearly visible. Of course, there is no one looking in. But I don't like the feeling. And I don't like it when I glance up and see those black windowpanes. I wish I could cover them, to stop the night peering in.

Over the weeks, I've struck up an acquaintance with the operator at the meteorological station on Bear Island. His name is Ohlsen. He's got a wife and two little girls in Bodø, and he misses them. But since the others left, I haven't wanted to chat. I don't like being on the bicycle generator with the head-phones on and my back to the room. I don't know what's happening behind me. Although of course, nothing is.

I'm worried about Gus. They'll still be en route to Longyearbyen. What if he gets worse and they have to operate on board? I forgot to tell Algie to wire me as soon as there's news, but he'll know to do that, won't he? Surely he'll know?

The weather remains clear and cold (minus twelve) and very still. Around ten in the morning, a pallid greenish glimmer appears in the south-east behind the cliffs: proof that somewhere, the sun still exists. To the north-west, it remains deep night. On a clear day like today, the twilight strengthens to pinkish gold, revealing every ridge of the mountains, making the icecap glow. You can't help thinking that dawn is coming — but no, soon it's getting dark again, the shadows already turning violet, the twilight fading to green. In time, it will fade to nothing.

And the worst of it is, when I'm inside, I can't *see* the twilight, because the cabin faces north-west, towards endless night.

24th October
··

I went to bed with a lamp on a chair, but I kept starting awake and checking that I hadn't knocked it over, so in the end I had to put it out. Then I had a horrible half-waking dream that there was someone in the bunk above mine. I saw the bulge of the mattress between the slats. I heard them creak. I woke with a jolt. Steeling myself, I got up and switched on my torch. Of course it revealed nothing but mounds of clothes.

I wish we'd thought to bring nightlights. I remember the exact entry in the Army & Navy Price List: *Clark's Pyramid Nightlights, 12s. 9d per dozen boxes, each one burns for 9 hrs.*

Surely the *Isbjørn* will have reached Longyearbyen by now. Maybe Gus has already had the operation. Maybe . . .

Stop it, Jack. Go and make breakfast. Porridge with a chunk of pemmican in it. Scones with gooseberry jam. That'll set you right.

Later
....

Another cold, windless day (minus fifteen), but overcast, so no twilight.

Out to sea there's a band of deepest charcoal which looks like bad weather, only I can't tell if it's advancing or receding. This stillness is getting on my nerves. Where are the blizzards we're supposed to have in the autumn?

Without daylight, terms such as "morning", "noon" and "night" have no meaning. And yet I cling to them. I impose them like a grid on the formless dark. I know that "evening" is merely the stretch between the transmission at half past five and the reading at seven in the "morning", but still I rub my hands and say briskly, "Now then, what shall we do this evening?"

All quiet today, nothing untoward to report. (I like the way that even in this journal, I can't bring myself to name it. I circle round it with euphemisms. "Untoward". What does that even mean? *Characterised by misfortune or annoyance. Not auspicious; un-favourable. Unseemly.* Unseemly. That's a good one. It certainly is that.)

Funny what you come across when you're not looking for it. Again I've gone through all our books on Spitsbergen, in case I missed something about what happened here. One of them was published in 1913; it describes Spitsbergen as a miner's paradise. Rich coal seams, easily dug. Deep anchorages. No taxes, no mining dues, no laws. *Each summer, a small army of prospectors and miners arrives from Russia, America, Germany, Norway, Britain. Disputes are frequent, and with no adjudicating authority, are summarily settled.* Settled how? Is that what this is about? A fight?

I couldn't find any mention of Gruhuken, but in another book there's a chapter on Spitsbergen folklore, which I've skipped. Damned if I'm going to let it put ideas in my head. I've got enough of those already.

In among Gus' volumes on botany and birds, I found a memorandum book bound in blue American cloth. I didn't know he'd been keeping a private journal, I thought he was making notes for the expedition report. It gave me such a jolt to see his handwriting. Sounds ridiculous, but I got all choked.

I put the journal back where I found it. Unread, of course.

25th October
....

AMAZING NEWS! A transmission from Longyearbyen! *GUS OP SUCCESS STOP ALL FINE STOP HAVE WIRED HIS PEOPLE STOP BEAR UP OLD CHAP BACK SOON STOP ALGIE STOP*

Thank *Christ.* I've only just realised that I've been carrying the anxiety inside me like a coiled spring.

106

When I received the transmission, I was so relieved that I could hardly take down the words. He's OK. He's going to be OK. In a few days he'll be back and it'll be as if he's never been away.

To celebrate, I laced my breakfast porridge with Golden Syrup and whisky. Then I came over all dutiful, and got the Austin going for the weekly dispatches to England. (Which is easier said than done, as it's a recalcitrant beast and dislikes the chill at this end of the cabin, so I pamper it by warming the valves in the oven.) I'm quite proud of my dispatch to *The Times*. I kept it matter-of-fact, business as usual: Expedition Leader temporarily indisposed, Wireless Operator taking over in the interim. I don't want them getting all sensational about me being here on my own.

It was a clear "day", with enough light at eleven to justify calling it that, so I took the dogs for a run on the beach.

My God, what would I do without them? They're the liveliest, most affectionate creatures. I love the sound of their paws pattering over the snow as they hurtle off to investigate things, then hurtle back to tell me about it. Upik isn't as fierce as I'd thought, but she is fearless; and her mate Svarten might be shy with me, but he certainly keeps the rest of his pack in line. Kiawak is also black, like Svarten, with long soft fur and tawny eyebrows; he hates getting his paws wet. Eli is creamy-white, and none too bright (I call him the Dumb Blond). Pakomi, Jens and Anadark have wolf colouring: shaggy grey-and-tan fur, tipped black at the ends. They're full of mischief, and love jumping on top

107

of the doghouse to survey the scene; I think they have designs on the cabin roof. Isaak also has wolf colouring, but a handsomer face than the others, and arresting light-blue eyes.

To think that I wanted to leave them behind. That I actually suggested shooting them.

Later

There's a thin film of ice on the bay.

I didn't notice when I was out with the dogs, but I saw it this evening after the five o'clock readings. It's *very* thin. When I threw a stone, it shattered into long, jingling slivers. The tide will disperse it. But I've got to face facts. At some stage, the sea is going to freeze over.

When?

I remember Eriksson talking about the colliers at Longyearbyen and how they only stop running some time in November. But Gruhuken is further north than Longyearbyen.

What if the sea freezes before Gus and Algie get back? What if I've got to stay here alone until spring?

26th October

Nothing happened, I just gave myself a fright. Stupid, stupid. I've got to watch that. An accident out here wouldn't be funny.

108

Another still day and very overcast, so no twilight. Six thirty in the "morning" and I'm letting the dogs out, when it starts to snow. Softly, insidiously, shutting out the world. No sea, no mountains, no sky. The dogs appear and disappear in the greyness like — well, like shadows. I bless Eriksson for making us put up those guide ropes.

But that bloody Stevenson screen. The louvres are supposed to protect the instruments from the sun, but since there isn't any, all they do is become crusted with frost, which has to be removed three times a day. The only way of doing that is to scrape it off with your knife, and it's damned awkward, partly because you're wearing snowshoes, which makes it tricky crouching down, and partly because you're screwing up your eyes against flying particles and your headlamp's shooting disconcerting beams into the gloom. You long to hear Gus crunching towards you through the snow. Hell, you'd even settle for Algie, whistling "All By Yourself in the Moonlight".

It happened just after the five o'clock reading. The dogs were off somewhere, but I knew they wouldn't have gone far, as it was less than an hour till feeding time. It was snowing hard, with a light, persistent wind making the flakes eddy and whirl.

I'd just finished at the screen, and was plodding back towards the cabin: my headlamp off, spindrift streaming towards me like fingers, and me hunched into the wind, with one hand on the guide rope. I could hear the rasp of my breath and the scrape of my snowshoes, and I made a point of not looking back. I don't when I'm in snowshoes, as I've learnt that they create a not very pleasant auditory illusion: you fancy you hear the scrape of *other* snowshoes, following right behind you. But of course it's simply the echo of your own.

I was wiping the snow from my eyes when I saw someone standing at the door.

I was so startled that my snowshoes crossed and I fell, bashing my hip on a rock.

And of course it wasn't anyone, it was only the bear post.

Stupid. What's the matter with you, Jack? Next you'll be scared of your own shadow! From now on, you watch your step, my lad. What if you'd broken your leg? What if you'd hit your head and knocked yourself out?

Later

It stopped snowing around six, and we're back to the stillness. The windless calm. Except it doesn't feel calm. You can have stillness without calm. Gruhuken has taught me that.

I find myself creeping about the cabin, taking care not to make too much noise. It's as if I don't want to attract the attention of — what? I think of those trappers in the cabin on Barents Island. *For terror of the deadness beyond.*

It's hard to concentrate on anything. Often I break off to trim the lamps. I replenish them when they're still three-quarters full. I keep checking my torch batteries, and when I go out, I don't rely on my headlamp, I have a torch in either pocket and take a Tilley lamp, too. Even then, I worry. If the battery fails. If I drop the lamp.

Until now, I hadn't understood the absolute need for light. I hadn't appreciated that there's an unbridgeable difference between a stretch of "twilight" every twenty-four hours, and nothing at all. Only an hour or so of twilight is enough to confirm normality. It allows you to say, *Yes, here is the land and the sea and the sky. The world still exists.* Without that — when all you can see out the window is black — it's frightening how quickly you begin to doubt. The suspicion flickers at the edge of your mind: maybe there is nothing beyond those windows. Maybe there is only you in this cabin, and beyond it the dark.

Fear of the dark. Until I came here, I thought that was for children; that you grew out of it. But it never really goes away. It's always there underneath. The oldest fear of all. What's at the back of the cave?

Eriksson was right. One mustn't think too much. Keep busy, walk every day, that's what he said. I've got to follow that to the letter. Especially the walks.

29th October
....

Three days of rain. So no twilight, no moon, no stars. And this is ice rain, colder than anything I've ever experienced.

111

Maybe I lost my nerve a little after that incident at the Stevenson screen, because I couldn't face my usual back-and-forth along the beach. Instead I've been taking my walks by going outside and circling the cabin, with one hand on the wall, so as not to get lost. I keep my headlamp on at all times.

Round and round I go, and by now I know every nail in the planking, every loose corner of tarpaper. Each circuit has its scares and reassurances. Turn right out of the door and head past the woodpile and the drums of paraffin and petrol. Past the outhouse and the coal dump, with the dog sledge propped against it. Then I'm off the boardwalk, but I don't mind, as this is the best bit because I've reached the doghouse. I undo the latch and out comes a flurry of whiskery muzzles and flailing paws. For a circuit or two they accompany me, then they get bored and scatter — although Isaak stays close for a while longer, probably because he knows I've brought him a butterscotch. Sometimes I keep him with me on a rope, but usually I don't have the heart to deprive him of his run, so I'm left alone.

Past the doghouse it's worse, because my mittened hand must leave the cabin wall and touch naked rock. As I near the end of the boulders, I slow, fearing what I might meet around the corner. I shout to scare off — what? Foxes? Bears? Although the pack ice must still be miles out to sea, so there's not much chance of bears, and with the dogs about, they're even less likely.

Now I'm past the boulders, and my hand finds the planks of the cabin again, and I'm back on the boardwalk. You'd think it'd be a relief, but I hate this end of the cabin, I can't forget that it's the site of the old trappers' hut. So I hurry, my gaze fixed on the blessed glimmer of the storm lantern hanging from the antlers over the porch. I try not to catch sight of the bear post, three paces from the door. I hate it if the beam of my headlamp cuts across it.

I reach the door and bang on it for luck. Well done, Jack. One circuit done. Only nineteen more to go.

Twenty circuits per day, that's my rule, and it must *not* be broken. Like the readings and transmissions, it's a peg on which my routine depends, a fixed point in my existence.

Drying out my gear has become another. I spend hours turning gloves inside out, hanging socks over the stove, checking that nothing has scorched. Every item of clothing is a trusted friend. This afternoon I had to stop myself talking to my muffler.

The stove is a friend, too, albeit a fickle one, and when it's windy, we have a love — hate relationship. I fuss over it and cajole it into doing better. I keep the door open and watch the flap of the flames, and praise the flaring hiss of a recalcitrant log. I swear at it when it refuses to burn.

I thought I was lonely back in London, but it was never like this. Lonely? I was among millions of people! Here I've got no one. I'm the only human being for

Shut *up*, Jack. This isn't helping.

Later

Message from Algie. *GUS WELL BUT DOC SAYS CAN'T COME FOR AT LEAST TWO WEEKS STOP SORRY OLD CHAP STOP*

Two weeks?

I've been pacing the cabin, trying to take it in. I've done a week on my own already. It feels like a month. How can I bear two more? And why did he say "at least"? What did he mean?

Two weeks. That's mid-November. Jesus. Will the sea still be clear by then? Will they be able to get through?

Whisky. Lots of it. That's the ticket.

30th October

I read that chapter on folklore. I wish I hadn't.

Most of it wasn't even about Spitsbergen, not specifically. It was just a rather dreary account of Scandinavian beliefs, some of which I recognise from old English customs. The idea that seabirds bring good luck when you're out fishing. And scattering salt to ward off witches; Mother used to do that when she ate a boiled egg, a pinch of salt over her shoulder. I'd forgotten.

It says that "some places in Spitsbergen" — it doesn't say which — are haunted by *draugs*. A *draug* is the unquiet spirit of a drowned man who lurks in the shallows, waiting to drag the unwary to their doom.

114

When a corpse is washed up, there is always a dilemma. If you bury it, are you cheating the sea of its due? If you do not, will you be haunted by the draug?

I like the "when". How often is a corpse washed up here, anyway?

And then there's this. *Those who know the islands maintain that the beginning of the polar night is a time for particular care. Some say that seven weeks before Yule, the graves of Spitsbergen open.*

Seven weeks from Christmas. That's October the 31st. Hallowe'en.

But Jack, so *what?*

When I was a boy, Father gave me a book called *Folk Tales from the North.* Most of the stories were about witches and trolls and ghosts playing havoc on All Hallows' Eve — which, when you think about it, is completely understandable, a natural response to living in the north. Of *course* you'd believe in things like that when you're facing a long dark winter, and the whole world feels dead.

But what you've got to remember is that there's nothing *new* in any of this. Nothing you didn't already know.

The 31st of October is tomorrow.

CHAPTER
TEN

....

Did I make it happen? Was I more "open" to perceiving it because of what I'd just read? Because of the date?

It snowed in the night. When I went to take the seven o'clock readings, it was warmer, only minus nine, and a clear "morning", thank God, the moon a brilliant crescent in an indigo sky prickling with stars. Fresh snow clothed the camp in weird grey radiance, and I could *see*: the pale curves of the whale bones on the beach, the icebergs on the sea. (The sea is mercifully unfrozen; I checked. From now on I'm going to keep an ice watch three times a day.)

I felt ashamed of my cowardice over the past few days. Those dismal circuits around the cabin, with me clinging to the walls — as if I'd be lost for ever if I didn't maintain contact. I can't let things affect me like this. Not with two more weeks to go.

So in a spirit of defiance, I took the dogs for a walk on the slopes behind camp.

To begin with it was beautiful. The dogs raced about, yelping, chasing each other. Isaak tugged on his rope — I'm training him to accompany me — but I was firm, and soon he was trotting along docilely; which was just as well, as I was wearing snowshoes and had a ski pole in either hand and a rifle over my shoulder.

As the twilight strengthened, we followed the frozen stream uphill, and I congratulated myself. See? All it takes is a bit of grit. And look how beautiful it is! The undulating white slopes, the glimmering peaks, the drooping heads of grasses poking through the snow. Even the mining ruins were transformed.

Isaak gave an excited *wuff* — and in the distance I made out black dots moving on white. Reindeer!

See? I told myself as I restrained an eager husky. There *is* life out here. You just need the guts to go and find it.

The dogs hurtled after the reindeer, which tilted back their heads and galloped off at surprising speed. The dogs quickly realised it was hopeless, and bounded back to me.

It was hard going uphill, and soon I was bathed in sweat. Climbing in snowshoes means digging in with your toes so that the spikes underneath can get a grip, and hauling yourself up with your ski poles till your elbows ache. And after all that rain there was ice under the snow, so each step made a glassy crunch — or an alarming scrape when I hit exposed rock — or a jolting *whump* in a drift.

One snowshoe came off, and I knelt to rebuckle it.

When I rose, the land had changed. The mountains floated above long drifts of fog. A gauzy curtain veiled the bay. As I watched, the fog thickened till I could only distinguish features by contrast: the inky sea against the lighter grey shore.

"Time we were getting home," I told Isaak, and we started back. He plodded ahead, glancing back at me from time to time as if to say, why so slow? I kept my eyes down, watching my footing.

When I looked again, the mountains were gone. Sea and camp had vanished, obliterated by fog. I felt its clammy chill on my face.

"Sooner we get home the better," I told Isaak. My voice sounded jittery in the stillness. And it was so very still.

Defiantly, I snapped on my headlamp. Isaak's shadow loomed: a monster dog. My light scarcely illumined a yard ahead of me, but it showed my tracks clearly enough, leading back to camp. The best thing about snowshoes is that they make such unmistakable tracks. An idiot could follow them.

I don't know how I lost the trail, but I did. In disbelief I looked about me. Gone. I took the torch from my pocket and tried that. No good. Like the headlamp, the beam scarcely lit a yard in front. And "beam" is too strong a word. It was more of a diffuse glow, dissolving into the grey.

Downhill, I told myself. That's the ticket.

But around me I saw only grey, and with all contrast gone, it was impossible to make out the lie of the land. I swayed. I couldn't tell up from down. I headed off again. My snowshoes slid on an icy patch. At the same moment, Isaak caught a scent and lunged forwards. I fell. The rope slipped out of my hand. He was gone.

"Isaak!" I shouted. My voice sounded muffled. He didn't come back.

Cursing, I groped for my ski poles and struggled to my feet. The fog pressed on me from all sides.

"Svarten! Upik! Anadark! Jens! *Isaak!*"

Nothing. I stumbled on.

No, Jack, this is the wrong way, you're going uphill.

I backtracked. But there were no recognisable features to backtrack *to*. By now my trail was a mess of churned snow, no use following that. I thought of the storm lantern hanging from the antlers above the porch, where I couldn't see it. I wished I'd had the sense to hang one behind the cabin, too.

Yanking off my headlamp and throwing back my hood, I strained for some sound to guide me. The sea was too far off, and the stream was frozen. I heard nothing but my own urgent breath.

Lost. Lost.

Inside my waterproofs, my sweat-soaked clothes chilled me to the bone. I willed myself to keep calm. Think logically. How do you tell up from down?

Answer: you kick the snow ahead. If you can see where it goes, there's level ground in front. If not, there's a drop.

Pulling up my hood, I refixed the headlamp. Which isn't as easy as it sounds when you're wearing mittens and your hands are shaking.

My mind darted in panic. I saw myself stumbling further and further from camp, heading blindly for the icecap, falling down some forgotten mineshaft.

I thought, when two days go by without any transmissions from me, Bear Island will raise the alarm. They'll send a search party from Longyearbyen. Two days later — ice permitting — they'll arrive. They'll find a deserted camp and desperate dogs. Next summer, maybe someone will find my bones. All this flashed through my mind in an instant.

Then I remembered the compass in my pocket. *Idiot*. All you've got to do is head north-east and you'll reach the sea.

I dropped the bloody thing in the snow. I scrabbled for it. Whipped off my mittens. Couldn't find it. Shit. *Shit*.

Found it. The arrow didn't move. Not broken, surely not broken?

I jiggled it. The arrow swung wildly. My hand was trembling, I couldn't hold the compass steady. I set it on a rock.

The arrow — the blessed little arrow — swung round — wavered — and went still. There. That way.

Gasping, I stumbled downhill. I passed a patch of snow dotted with tufts of light-brown hair where a reindeer had rested, and this sign of life heartened me immensely. A few paces on, my headlamp caught the bright yellow spots of a dog's frozen urine. Then I heard the distant yowls of huskies.

Thirty paces more took me to the beach.

"Jesus," I whispered. "*Jesus*."

In my wanderings I'd strayed a long way off course, and had fetched up at the eastern end of the bay, under the cliffs. Sagging with relief and ashamed of my panic, I turned my back on the cliffs and started along the shore, keeping close to the water for fear of losing myself again.

The humped bulk of the emergency storehouse loomed out of the fog. Then the whale bones, glittering in the beam of my headlamp. At last I made out the bear post — and beyond it the miraculous glimmer of the lantern over the porch.

I shouted for the dogs. "Upik! Pakomi! Anardark! Eli! Isaak!"

No response. But that was OK; they'd come back when they were hungry. Eagerly, I hurried on.

As I approached the bear post, my headlamp lit the cairn of rocks at its base, where a tuft of dead grass poked through the snow. The light touched the weathered grey wood of the post. Fog had darkened the blotchy stains to black.

The dread came from nowhere. Without warning, my flesh began to crawl. I felt the hairs on my scalp prickle and rise. I couldn't see anything except the bear post and its cairn of stones, but my body braced itself. It knew.

Then, through the fog on the other side of the post, came an odd, muffled scraping. A sound as of metal dragged over rock.

Jerkily I turned, the beam of my headlamp sweeping the fog. I saw nothing. And yet that sound was louder, more distinct. Clink. Clink. Coming closer. Towards me.

My heart hammered in my throat. I tried to run. My legs wouldn't move.

It was in front of me now, the sound only a few feet away — and still I saw nothing. This can't be. But I hear it.

Clink. Clink.

Silence.

It had reached the post. It was so close that if I could have moved, I might have reached out my hand and touched — what? A presence. Unseen. Unbearably close.

I stood helpless, not breathing, my arms clamped to my sides. Dread rising within me, a black tide drowning . . .

Behind me, the patter of paws.

With a moan I broke free. I staggered back. My snowshoes crossed. I fell.

Isaak ran into the beam of my headlamp and stopped, ears pricked, tail tautly raised. His eyes gleamed silver, throwing back my light.

As I got to my knees, he came towards me, lashing his tail. In his silvered eyes I saw the twin reflections of a dark round head.

It took a moment to recognise myself.

CHAPTER
ELEVEN

I found my way to the porch. Yanked open the door and slammed it behind me. Dragged off my outer things. Stumbled down the hall. The bunkroom. The main room. My torch beam sliced the dark. My breath smoked.

I tried to light a lamp, but my hands were shaking too hard. I found a handful of birch bark and threw it in the stove with a couple of logs. At last I got them to take. I crouched, staring at the flames between my fingers. In my head I still heard that sound. Still felt that presence.

My teeth were chattering, my clothes soaked in freezing sweat. I blundered back to the bunkroom, snatched dry things, undressed and dressed in front of the stove. I found a bottle of Scotch and splashed some in a mug and gulped it down.

The whisky steadied me. I managed to light a lamp. And another and another. Suddenly I was ravenous. I made coffee and porridge. I gobbled it like a starving man. I ran to the slops pail and retched.

I longed to hear voices. Normality. I tried the wireless. The receiver needed charging. Cursing, I pedalled the bicycle generator, not looking at the windows. I tuned in to the Empire programme. A play. The clink of teacups, the brittle chatter of women.

I went to the north window and put my hands to the glass and peered out. The dogs were back: some curled up with their tails over their noses, some quietly chewing snow. All seemed oblivious of the bear post.

It stood three yards from the window. I told myself it was only a log. A stick of driftwood.

I went and sat at the table. My mouth was bitter with bile. I had heard those sounds. I had felt that presence. I had not imagined them.

The radio play ended. The calm, efficient voice of the BBC announced the next programme.

My wristwatch told me it was ten o'clock. I'd set out on the walk at eight. Only two hours? How was that possible? It felt like years.

I needed something to still the panic. Something to make the sounds go away.

Lurching to my feet, I blundered to the bookshelf, found Gus' journal, and opened it. To hell with respecting his privacy. I needed him.

The sight of his handwriting instantly gave me courage. It was round and schoolboyish, and he'd been so enthusiastic that at times he'd scored the paper. He'd filled pages with nature descriptions — birds, molluscs, plants — interspersed with reflections on the Arctic and on the characters of Norwegian sealers. I devoured it all, the more boring the better.

As I'd expected, he kept mostly to facts, with little emotion; presumably that's beaten out of you at Harrow. He was largely silent about Algie, although he

124

mentioned me a few times, and of course I pounced on that.

I don't think Jack likes Algie very much, he'd written on the 31st of July, the day we saw Spitsbergen for the first time. *Whenever Algie says something crass, which God knows is often enough, I can see Jack's jaw tightening. I think it's a physical effort for him not to slap Algie down. It's really rather funny.* That made me smile. Gus had noticed almost before I'd realised myself.

Then, shortly after we'd arrived at Gruhuken, he remarked on my dislike of the mining remains. *Jack has such intense responses to things, it must make life hard for him. And yet I do understand why he doesn't like the "past poking through" as he puts it, because I'm the same. I want Gruhuken to be ours, and ours alone.*

I was surprised, and gratified. I didn't know he'd felt the same way.

A few pages on, I came across a passage about Eriksson which I found vaguely unsettling. *What an admirable fellow. Born to abject poverty on a farm in the Tronds; as children they went barefoot from May to October (in north Norway!). Stowed away aged ten, never went back. No schooling, taught himself to read from the Bible. Deep regard for his ship and crew, if too reserved to admit it. Thoughtful, resilient, polite, unforgiving. Superstitious, too. This afternoon he had a pail of fish entrails thrown overboard to attract gulls: like many seamen, he believes they bring good luck and ward off evil. Algie laughed. I told him for Christ's sake not to let Eriksson hear. I grew up with people like Mr E. Country people: devout Christians, but scratch the surface and you find some pretty rum beliefs. The funny thing is, there's often something in them.*

Why had Gus seen fit to record that? And the date. The 9th of August. By then we'd been at Gruhuken a week.

A day later, this: *In one of my books it says that parts of Spitsbergen are haunted. I asked Mr E, but he wouldn't say yes or no. He said (and I translate from his less idiomatic phrasing): "Up here a man becomes aware of things that he can't perceive further south."*

Bafflingly, Gus made no further comment on this, but launched straight into two pages of nature notes. I've noticed that about him. He seems to have the ability to detach himself completely from anything disagreeable: to exclude it and immerse himself in something else. Maybe that's another skill he acquired at Harrow.

31st August. This place isn't right. I've felt it ever since the Isbjørn *left.*

What? What?

That time in the canoe when I watched the kelp moving in the water. I saw such things.

Christ. Christ, Gus, what did you see? Feverishly, I turned the pages. Nothing but bird behaviour and character studies of the dogs.

I can't believe it. All that time — weeks of living together — and he knew?

126

16th September. Why hasn't Jack felt anything? Last night we saw our first Aurora. I started to tell him, I wanted to. But he got that severe look and changed the subject. Can he really have sensed nothing? Of the three of us he's the strongest, the most pragmatic and level-headed. And yet he's perceptive, too, and has plenty of imagination. After all, he was moved almost to tears at his first sight of Gruhuken — and so concerned about an abandoned guillemot chick that he went back and spent ages trying to find it. So it's odd that he should be the only one who has noticed nothing.

The only one? Oh, surely not Algie . . .

10th October. Poor Algie. This morning I dragged him off for a walk, and he confessed everything. He said, "I know it sounds the most fearful rot, but this place is giving me the pips. There are times when I feel sort of — watched. And once, on those rocks, I had the most dreadful thought. Or rather, not a thought, but an image in my head. I saw knives. I don't want to say any more. And I smelt paraffin, I swear I did. I was desperate to get away but I couldn't move, it was as if I were bound hand and foot. That image is still in my head, I can't seem to get rid of it. It's absolutely beastly.

Now that winded me. Not fat, insensitive Algie, who whistled "Someone To Watch Over Me" on his first encounter with the Northern Lights.

A scrawled entry for the 14th of October. *This morning Algie told me he's started to hear things. He calls it a "waking nightmare". I badgered him for details, then wished I hadn't. I refuse to write them down. They're too horrific. And what unsettles me most is that they closely resemble what I experienced in the canoe. Poor Algie, he's in a frightful funk. And so ashamed. He made me swear not to tell Jack. I don't think I could even if I wanted to. Besides, I don't want Jack thinking I'm in a funk, too.*

I skimmed the remaining pages, but there was nothing more until just before Gus fell ill. *I've begun to realise,* he wrote on the 18th, *that prolonged darkness can affect the mind in ways I'd never anticipated. There's a lifeless stillness about this land which affects one shockingly. Perhaps I'm developing nerve strain, or that disorder the old trappers used to get. What did Jack call it?* Rar? *The extraordinary thing is that what I experienced in the canoe felt so intensely* real. *But of course it wasn't. No doubt that's in the nature of hallucinations, that they seem so real. After all, one's dreams feel real, even though they're merely artefacts of one's mind; and if my brain can create such "pseudo-reality" while I'm asleep, surely it's capable of performing the same trick while I'm awake? And yet — to say that all this is an hallucination — how is that a comfort? To know that my own mind can create such horrors.*

That was almost the last entry. The next day, he fell ill.

I sat stunned, staring at his writing on the page.

Oh, Gus. You were going through all that, and I didn't know. For your sake, I'm glad you're safe in the infirmary at Longyearbyen; but if only I'd known. We could have talked of it. We could have borne it together, made sense of it.

And yet if you were here now, Gus, and God knows I wish you were, I'd tell you that you're wrong. Whatever you experienced, you didn't imagine it. And there are worse things than hallucinations.

I don't believe for a moment that what I heard at the bear post was an "artefact of my mind". It had objective reality. It was an auditory imprint, a lingering trace of some act of savagery which was once perpetrated here at Gruhuken.

An act of savagery.

Why did I write that? Why, on the strength of the clink of metal over rock?

Because of the dread I felt. I wouldn't have felt that dread if something appalling hadn't happened here.

Writing that has put me in mind of something I haven't thought about in years. And I don't want to think about it now, so I *won't*. I'll take my lead from Gus. I refuse to write it down.

On the kitchen shelf, his alarm clock tells me that it's twenty to twelve. Time to go out for the twelve o'clock readings. I have to do it. Otherwise it's won.

But *what* has won?

Steady on, Jack, you're in danger of creating a monster out of shadows. Whatever it is, what you *must* remember is that it's in the past. Something happened here once. Something terrible. But whatever it was, *it's in the past*. Whatever you experienced was only an echo.

It was simply an echo.

CHAPTER
TWELVE

31st October, later

....

I did go out at noon, and again at five. Both times, the dogs gave me a rapturous welcome and came with me to the Stevenson screen. They seemed completely at ease. I found that intensely reassuring.

I haven't been near the bear post since it happened. To reach the screen I took the back way, turning right out of the porch and looping round behind the cabin. I'm going to do that from now on.

A few minutes ago I went to the window. I saw the shadowy shapes of the dogs, peacefully gnawing chunks of seal in front of the cabin. A light wind from the icecap is blowing spindrift over them, but they don't seem to mind. I haven't tied them to their stakes. I don't see the point. They're not going to run away. And like this they can warn me of bears.

It's such a normal sight. Inside, too, everything's normal. Bright lamps, crackling stove. A whisky at my elbow, one of Hugo's cigars between my teeth. When I look at myself in the shaving mirror, I see no horror, no fear. Nothing to connect me with the wild-eyed man who was retching into the slops pail a few hours ago.

What I've got to remember is that others have overwintered here and they too must have experienced

130

things — *but they managed.* Well, so shall I. I won't let this beat me.

So I've decided on a few ground rules.

First. I'll no longer kennel or tether the dogs, but will let them roam freely around camp. I'll wedge the door of the doghouse open, so that they can come and go as they please, but still have shelter. I don't think they'll come to any harm. They were bred for the Arctic.

Second. I'll draw up a ration plan. It'd be unthinkable if Gus and Algie return to find that I'd squandered our supplies.

Third. I'll cut down on the drinking. (OK, that one starts tomorrow.)

Fourth. No more than nine hours' sleep a night. In this endless dark, one can easily sleep twelve hours or more — but that must be resisted. I *have* to maintain a structure. Sleeping time, eating time, work time. That's the ticket.

Seeing these rules, neatly numbered on the page, is extraordinarily comforting.

And it's good to know that outside there are eight watchful huskies patrolling the camp.

1st November

A good day. I slept the regulation nine hours without dreaming, and was woken by Gus' alarm clock.

My new rules are working. When I'm not busy with the usual tasks, I'm tiring myself out with new ones: cleaning, laundry, weather proofing the doghouse with tarpaper

131

securely tamped down and lots of straw bedding inside. I check the bay for ice (so far, thank God, it's clear). And when I'm in the cabin, I keep the wireless on. I have chats in Morse with Ohlsen on Bear Island. And this afternoon I "spoke" to Algie again. He told me that Gus is doing well, and I told him about my new rules (but not that I'm letting the dogs run wild). Twice he asked if I'm "all right", and I said I'm fine. Stonewalling him gave me a perverse kind of pleasure. If he wants to keep things on the surface, then so will I. He knows what kind of place this is. He knows what he fled and I didn't.

But what does that matter? My rules are working, that's the point.

Things would be back to normal if it wasn't for a ridiculous habit I've developed of peering out of the north window to check on the bear post. It's ludicrous, I know, but I need to reassure myself that it isn't quite as close to the cabin as I'd thought.

Of course each time I look it's exactly where it ought to be, a good three paces from the window. But here's the irritating thing: afterwards, when I've been busy on something else, the doubt creeps back. In my mind's eye the post is closer, and nearer the door, as if it's about to gain entry. I know that's preposterous, but I still have to go to the window and make sure. Which means that whatever I'm doing, the wretched thing is never far from my thoughts.

Outside it's minus nine, with a south wind hissing over the snow. The barometer is falling. I wonder if we're in for a storm?

When I "spoke" to Algie, I asked if there was any change to when they'd be coming back. He said no, but he didn't go into detail. Previously, he'd said "at least two weeks". That was on the 29th of October. Which means they'll get here on the 12th of November — at the earliest. Eleven days from now. If I stick to my rules, I might be able to hold out till then.

Just now, I made my last check before turning in.

There's a bright crescent moon. The bear post casts a long, thin shadow, reaching towards me.

If only I couldn't see the bloody thing at all.

2nd November

I was finishing breakfast when it occurred to me that since waking up, I'd already checked the post at least a dozen times.

That did it. I slammed down my mug. "Bloody hell! This has got to stop!"

Running to the bunkroom, I grabbed an armful of blankets and hurried about, tacking them over the windows. There. You've been moaning about having no curtains. Well now you do.

It worked for about an hour. Then I drew back a corner and peered out.

And of course the post was where it's always been: a little closer than I'm comfortable with, but no more and no less than it was before.

From now on, I'm going to try an alternative strategy: acknowledge the obsession, but limit it. You're allowed ten checks a day — *and no more.*

I've left the "curtains" in place, though. I can pin them back if there's anything to see, but for now, they're a distinct improvement.

The wind is moaning in the stovepipe, and somewhere a corner of tarpaper is flapping. I'll have to see to that.

Later

I've just come in from the five o'clock readings and I don't know what to make of it.

The readings themselves were straightforward. Decent weather, minus ten and still the wind blowing from the icecap, but the sky is clear, with a spectacular display of the Northern Lights. The camp, the shore, the icebergs in the bay — all were bathed in that wondrous pale-green light. I no longer find them intimidating. They're reassuring. After all, they're merely a physical phenomenon: the result of particles from solar flares bombarding the atmosphere.

The dogs bounded up to greet me — they're taking to their new-found freedom wonderfully well — and I fed them some brandy balls. Then, whistling through my teeth (shades of Algie!), I trudged round the back of the cabin to the Stevenson screen. Isaak came with me and I gave him some butterscotch (as he knew I would). He came back with me too, and we followed the guide rope to the radio masts, then looped behind the cabin. We'd turned the corner past the

134

outhouse and were heading for the porch when something brought me up short.

Surely the bear post was slightly closer than before?

Isaak nosed my thigh, wondering why I'd stopped. I ignored him and took out my torch. He looked up at me and doubtfully wagged his tail. Emboldened by his presence, I walked to the north window, then turned and paced from there to the bear post and back. Two and a half paces. Only two and a half. Before, it was three.

Unless I'd unwittingly lengthened my stride, which is perfectly possible. But I couldn't bring myself to try again.

Back in the cabin, I had a stiff drink, a couple of cigarettes, and a stern talk with myself. Logs don't move on their own. The fact that the bear post *appeared* closer is because it was easier to see, and that's because of the Northern Lights.

My conscious mind accepts this. But the deeper part — the part which remembers the darkness of the caves — wonders if I might be wrong.

3rd November
....

What utter rubbish I wrote last night. "The darkness of the caves"! I've been letting that bloody thing get to me. It's got to stop.

Well, it certainly has now.

Today was awful. When I wasn't peering through the window, I was telling myself *not* to look; which meant that even when I was doing something else it was constantly on my mind. It was so exhausting that after lunch I had to take a nap.

I woke at three, bleary and thick-headed. The first thing I did was drag myself to the window for another check.

I was about to peel back the curtain when I realised what I was doing. Christ, Jack, if you keep on like this, you'll lose your mind.

"I'm not having this!" I shouted. *"I'm not having it!"*

Dragging on my clothes, I grabbed a torch and an axe and flung myself out into the dark.

The dogs surged about me, sensing that something was up.

"I'm not having it," I panted.

I kept saying it over and over, like a protective charm, as I swung the axe and chopped the bloody thing down. I aimed low, to avoid the dark stains higher up, I didn't want my axe touching them. The post was hard as granite. It didn't want to be chopped down. The dogs stood behind me in a huddle, silent for once. When at last the post groaned and crashed into the snow, they raced off with their tails between their legs.

Panting, chest heaving, I hacked the wretched thing to chunks. I left them lying in the snow. There. That's one lot of driftwood I *won't* be adding to the woodpile. The thought of letting it inside the cabin is utterly repellent.

I've just looked out of the north window. Good. Very good. Nothing but a snowy curve down to the sea. I can't even see the pieces. And it's begun to snow, so

136

soon they'll be obliterated. It'll be as if that bloody post never existed.

I should have done this weeks ago. I can't imagine why I didn't.

Later
....

The storm blew up an hour after I chopped down the post. Thick snow whirling, wind howling and rapping at the windows.

My first thought was that I'd summoned it. I'd loosed the demon of the storm. Good old cause and effect, the human instinct to jump to conclusions. It's nice to know that my powers of reasoning aren't much better than those of a savage.

My next thought was the dogs. This storm could last a while. What do I do? I can't bring them inside, they'd wreck the place. I'd better feed them now, before it gets any worse. As for water, they'll have to make do with snow. At least there's plenty of that.

We keep the dog food in the roof space above the hall, where the seal meat stays frozen. Thanks to Algie, there's plenty of that, as well as crates and crates of dog pemmican. Cramming hunks of seal meat in a sack, I opened the door — and the wind hit me like a fist. Flying ice scoured my face (I'd forgotten my balaclava helmet). Bent double, I battled along the boardwalk, the wind screaming in my ears and tearing at my clothes. Through the slit of the doghouse doorway, my torchlight revealed snowy mounds that erupted as I

137

flung in the meat. The dogs seemed unfazed by the storm, and delighted at their early meal.

Fuel, I thought as I struggled back. Logs and a drum of paraffin.

It took hours to drag it all into the hall. Then I had to clear away the snow that had found its way in, too.

It's nearly midnight, and still the blizzard is battering the cabin. It's flinging snow at the windows like pebbles, and moaning in the stovepipe. It's making every plank creak and groan. God, I hope the roof stays on. I hope the windows hold. The shutters are in the emergency store at the other end of the bay. Might as well be in Timbuktu.

But in a strange way, I welcome the storm. It's a known, physical force: a rush of snow-laden air, generated by pressure differentials. These are things I can understand. And it's better than the stillness.

6th November
....

Three days and no let-up. The storm never stops for an instant. The din is indescribable, a booming like a train, a wailing in the stovepipe. I'm finding it rather tiring. Even when I'm asleep, I dream of trams rattling and screeching. I can't remember what silence is like.

I can understand why the Vikings believed in storm giants. I keep having to remind myself that there is no intention behind this. It feels so angry. As if it wants to tear apart the cabin and carry me off into the night.

Reaching the Stevenson screen is out of the question, but I've kept up my contact with Ohlsen on Bear Island (thank God the wireless masts have held firm). In my transmissions I affect a seasoned old campaigner calm. *"IT'S A BIG ONE STOP SNOW UP TO WINDOWS STOP TIME TO CATCH UP ON MY READING!* I exchange messages with Algie, and through him with Gus. *BIT OF A BLOW STOP SCREEN MUST TAKE ITS CHANCES STOP AT LEAST IT'S KEEPING THE BAY FREE OF ICE STOP DOGS FINE STOP I THINK THEY LIKE IT!* Algie's replies are jaunty and Boy Scoutish. *JOLLY GOOD SHOW JACK! WE KNOW IT TAKES MORE THAN A BIT OF A BREEZE TO SHAKE YOUR NERVE!* You're right about that, Algie old chap. Unlike you, I'm not one to get in a blue funk because of a few bad dreams. But then you know that already, don't you, old man?

Clinging to my routine, I take my walks *inside* the cabin, making careful circuits about the main room and berating myself if I lose count and have to start all over again. Which I often do.

I try once a day to take food to the dogs, but in reality it's more like every other day, so when I do, I give them lots, to make up for it. Each time I have to chop away the wind-packed snow blocking their doorway. They seem all right, if a bit cowed, but I worry. What if they suffocate? What if I can't get to them and they eat each other? When I'm in the cabin, I talk to them through the bunkroom wall — or rather,

I shout — and they yowl back. At least then I know they're still alive.

To think there was a time when I actually liked snow. It's horrible. Stinging your eyes. Blinding you, leading you astray. Each time I open the door I let in a whirlwind, and have to spend ages clearing it up (although I admit that this helps keep the water barrel full). And still the snow finds its way in, sifting under doors and through hidden cracks I never knew existed. Frost is beginning to crust the inside walls of the cabin and gather under the bunks. You wouldn't think it could get as far as the main room, but it does. I spend hours scraping it off. Mopping up damp, drying towels over the stove.

That stove. Before, it was merely temperamental. Now it's diabolical; although I can still get it to light if I splash the logs with paraffin. But three times — *three times* — a particularly savage gust of wind has blown a great cloud of smoke down the stovepipe and out into the cabin. Which leaves me black as a chimney sweep, coughing up my lungs, with hours of cleaning ahead. That's the storm's vicious little joke. Ha ha ha. Despite my efforts, the walls are now grimy with soot. It's got into the wood, I can't scrub it clean.

To cheer myself up, I flouted my ration plan this evening and put our Christmas bottles of champagne to cool in the porch.

To cool? Jack, have you gone daft?

Both bottles froze within minutes, and burst with a sound like a rifle report. I picked out the broken glass

140

and salvaged what I could: a large bowl of frozen mush. I've been eating it with a spoon. It's delicious.

Bit strong, though. Whoops. Jack you're drunk. Or "tipsy", as Gus would say. Off to bed with you.

8th November

Six days and still blowing.

Four days to go till Gus and Algie get back. Although that's only my guess, and Algie did say "at least" two weeks. And if the storm keeps up, they wouldn't even set out.

That champagne was too much for me, I went down like a stunned ox. Bit of a sick headache this morning, but Algie's Effervescing Morning Powder put me to rights.

You're prevaricating, Jack. Out with it.

As soon as I got up, I went to the north window and peered into the swirling grey. The bear post was back.

Feverishly I rubbed my breath off the glass. There it was. Straight. Tall. Not possible. You chopped it down. You hacked it to pieces with an axe.

The storm must have thrown up another log from the shore. But then why does it stand so upright and still? And isn't it closer than before, and a little to the right? Nearer the porch?

A gust of extraordinary violence struck the window, and I drew back. When I looked again, the post was gone. All I saw was snow, twisting in columns in the screaming wind. There was no post. There never was a post.

That was five hours ago. Since then I've managed to get a sack of seal meat to the dogs. I've told Bear Island that I'm fine. I've eaten a tin of boiled mutton and another of pears. And I've smoked a whole packet of Player's.

I've also flicked through this journal, which was a mistake. I'm shocked at how my handwriting's changed. I used to write a neat copperplate hand, but since I've been alone, it's degenerated into a spidery scrawl. Without reading a word, you can see the fear.

When the storm blew up, I wrote that I welcomed it. All that about pressure differentials and things I can understand. Bollocks. The constant din, the screaming fury. It's wearing me down. Grinding away my defences.

9th November

I woke to silence. Unbroken, unbelievable silence. Not a whisper of wind disturbing the peace.

The blanket over the bunkroom window had come down, and I was lying in moonlight. The windowpanes were silver squares criss-crossed with black. Putting out my hand, I felt the light seeping into my skin. I was an underwater swimmer, floating in light. Beautiful, beautiful light. I was so grateful I wanted to cry.

At last, disentangling myself from my sleeping bag, I pulled on my clothes and padded to the window.

There before me hung the full moon: huge, shining, golden. Every detail of camp lay sparklingly revealed. Where the bear post had been, I saw only a gentle curve of snow.

Like a recovering invalid, I shuffled about the cabin, tearing down blankets to let in the moon. I got the stove going. I didn't light any lamps. I didn't want anything to diminish that miraculous light.

Soon I would go out and tend to the dogs and see if the Stevenson screen was still there, but not yet. The moon drew me. I wanted to gaze and gaze. I hated to waste a moment.

At the north window, I cupped my hands to a pane and peered out.

The storm had cleared the ice from the bay. The moon cast a path of beaten silver over the sea, leading away from Gruhuken. "Beautiful," I murmured. "Beautiful . . ."

I watched it rise higher. I watched it gradually change from gold to silver, losing none of its brilliance. My breath misted the pane. I cleared it with my sleeve. When I looked again, a thin haze of cloud had dimmed the moon to inky blue.

At that moment, I sensed I was not alone.

With my nose pressed to the window, I felt horribly vulnerable, but I couldn't pull away. I had to look.

Where the bear post had been, a figure was standing.

Around it the snow glimmered faintly; but no light touched what faced me. It cast no shadow.

It stood utterly still, watching me. In one appalling heartbeat I took in its wet round head and its arms

143

hanging at its sides, one shoulder higher than the other. I felt its will coming at me in waves. Intense, unwavering, malign. Such malevolence. No mercy. No humanity. It belonged to the dark beyond humanity. It was rage without end. A black tide drowning.

And still I pressed my hands against the pane. I couldn't pull away. A dreadful communion.

I don't know how long I stood there. At last I had to breathe, and the pane misted over. When I'd cleared it, the figure was gone.

I ran to the west window and peered out. Nothing. The radio masts mocked my terror. I ran to the bunkroom window. Again nothing. I ran back into the main room and halted to listen. All I heard was the painful thudding of my heart.

The clouds had cleared, and once again the moon shone bright. The snow in front of the cabin was smooth. Innocent. Nothing to show that something had stood there. But it had. It had. I had felt its will. Its malevolence beating at me.

At me.

I've been wrong, wrong, wrong.

This is no echo.

CHAPTER
THIRTEEN

I stood three feet from the window, staring at my reflection in the pane.

If only I could believe that what I'd seen had been myself. But when you see yourself in a dark window, you see *yourself*: your own face and build. What I'd seen had had no unkempt beard, no wild hair sticking up all over its head. It had no face.

What is it? What does it want? Why is it angry with me? Is it because I destroyed the hut? What can I do to appease it?

Behind me, a crackle of static. The lights of the Eddystone flickered to life. I must have switched it on as I hurried about taking down blankets from the windows, although I didn't remember. And yet there it was. A transmission.

My knees buckled. *A transmission.* Was that what I'd just experienced? Something forcing its way through, like blood staining a bandage?

From the doghouse came urgent yowls. *The storm's over! We're hungry!*

In a cracked voice I called to them that I was coming soon.

Once again, tatters of inky cloud were drifting towards the moon, like a hand reaching to cover it.

Without taking my eyes from that bright, bruised face, I put on the head-phones and grabbed my notepad. I had to keep watching the moon. If I didn't, clouds would hide it again and then . . .

GUS HERE STOP

Gus?

Against doctor's orders, he'd made Algie take him to the wireless station.

My hand shook as I tapped an inadequate reply. *HOW ARE YOU?*

SORE BORED CROSS HOW ARE YOU?

FINE STOP

REALLY?

My finger paused on the key. *YES REALLY*, I replied. *BAD DREAMS BUT BETTER NOW STOP*

The answer came in a swift staccato rattle. *JACK ARE YOU ALL RIGHT? MR E IS HERE CAN FETCH YOU IN TWO DAYS STOP*

NO AM FINE STORM LONG BUT FINE NOW STOP

Why did I say that? Why not, *YES COME QUICK I CAN'T BEAR IT?*

Because it was Gus at the other end. Gus the golden-haired prefect whom Jack the eager schoolboy is so desperate to impress.

JACK YOU'RE AMAZING! AM SO TERRIBLY GRATEFUL! EXPEDITION SCUPPERED WITHOUT YOU!

146

I flushed with pleasure. Gus knew what I was braving to be here on my own; he knew what he owed me. I basked in his gratitude and admiration.

Now he was asking about the dogs.

DOGS SPLENDID, I replied. *AM V GLAD HAVE THEM ESP ISAAK RIPPING HOUND STOP*

As I tapped out my message, my eyes began to sting. It was so wonderful talking to Gus, but it hurt. It made me miss him even more.

JACK YOU MUFF I KNEW YOU LIKED THEM STOP

YES STOP

IDIOT STOP

YES STOP

I sat there grinning through my tears. It felt so good to have him tease me. So normal and warm and human.

On and on we talked, inconsequential chat, but everything to me. At last he said he had to go. I couldn't think of anything to delay him, so we agreed when next to speak, and said our goodbyes.

I switched off the receiver and stared at my printed notes of his words.

Talking to him had changed everything. It made me even more sharply aware of my isolation, but it also gave me strength. I was no longer the frightened obsessive who'd cowered in the storm and fought an illusory battle with a log. I was Jack Miller, the man who's keeping the 1937 Spitsbergen Expedition alive against all the odds.

I sat straighter. I took satisfaction in the cabin's every mundane detail. The orderly tins of powdered egg and

Breakfast Cocoa on the kitchen shelves. The clean steel lines of the bicycle generator. I felt the roughness of the table beneath my palms, I sniffed the familiar smells of paraffin, woodsmoke and unwashed clothes. This is my world. Modern. Practical. Real.

Realising I was ravenous, I tore open a bar of chocolate and wolfed it down. The sweetness burned my mouth, the rush of energy made me giddy. I brewed coffee and gulped two scalding mugs. I made a vast bowl of scrambled eggs with sausages and cheese. I lit lamps and tuned the wireless to the BBC. I revelled in each prosaic task.

Just now, I went to the bunkroom window. The sea is black and dotted with icebergs, but they're few and far between. I was right, the storm has kept the bay open. The dogs have dug their way out of the doghouse and are bounding about in the snow. Near the cabin, the drifts are almost to the window, but a few yards off it's shallower, and their paws don't sink in too far. When they saw me, they lashed their tails and yowled at me to come out. They wouldn't do that if there was anything there. Animals sense these things, don't they?

But it will be back. I know this. I carry that knowledge inside me like a stone.

What does it want? What terrible thing happened here to make it haunt with such malevolence?

I think of all the savagery I've ever heard about. I remember Algie's love of killing. His indifference to that seal's agony, his willingness to mutilate the dogs.

What happened here?

Later

I can't believe I was so stupid.

When I was "talking" to Gus, I was so overwhelmed that I forgot to ask the all-important question: when are you coming back?

And why didn't he say anything of his own accord?

The 12th of November. By my calculation, that's the soonest they'll arrive. It's three days away. But surely if they'd been about to set off, Gus would have said something. What isn't he telling me? How much longer have I got to hold on?

I have to go out again. The sky is clear. There's no cloud to cover the moon.

10th November

Yesterday feels like a millions years ago. I remember nerving myself with a shot of whisky and a cigarette to go outside. Then opening the door to a wall of snow.

God, I was relieved. Here was a physical task I could cope with.

The dogs heard me digging and set up an impatient clamour. I hacked my way though and they fell on me, lots of eager muzzles and flailing paws.

When at last I could look about me, I found Gruhuken transformed. The moon shone almost as bright as day. The snow was dazzling. Around me the camp lay radiant and serene. *Serene*. I felt not a trace of dread. No taint of that malign presence. The moon had banished it.

Buckling on my snowshoes, I made my way down to the shore, the dogs bounding along, vying for my attention. Moonlight turned the mountains to pewter. In the bay, icebergs glowed. At the water's edge, little black waves rimmed with grey foam lapped the shore. I breathed in great lungfuls of clean, freezing air. I felt the light soaking into my consciousness, dispelling the shadows from the deepest recesses of my brain. Whatever had come in the dark couldn't harm me in the light.

I worked for hours. First, I fetched tin after tin of pemmican for the dogs. Then I cleared the boardwalk and shovelled a path round the back of the cabin, another to the emergency store, and another to the Stevenson screen — which by some miracle has survived intact. As I worked, it occurred to me that somewhere beneath me lay the remains of the bear post. It belonged to another time. It had lost its power to terrify.

The *luxury* of working in light! And the moon stayed with me all the time. Gruhuken is so far north that when the moon is full, it doesn't set, but circles endlessly in the sky, so that you never lose sight of it. It's a miracle. A gift from the gods. Whenever you look up, there it is, watching over you.

Having finished my paths, I cleared the Stevenson screen and the other instruments, and collected my first set of data since the storm. I transmitted them to Bear Island. I got the Austin going and sent a report to

150

England (I'd skipped that during the storm). Then I went and stood in front of the porch and smoked a cigarette, like a settler in the old American West, surveying his homestead. I had regained possession of my camp. *My* camp. Jack Miller's.

The dogs had been playing on the shore, but suddenly Upik skittered to a halt and pricked her ears. One by one, the others did the same.

Had they caught the scent of a bear? I was about to fetch my gun when Svarten gave a low bark and hurtled west. The rest of the pack raced after him. As the patter of paws receded, I heard what they had heard: a scraping sound, echoing in the stillness. Scrape . . . scrape . . . scrape . . . Regular, long drawn out. But this was utterly different from the sound I'd heard at the bear post. This sound belonged to *my* world.

The dogs came rushing back, their eyes bright with excitement. Behind them, grey against the snow, I made out the figure of a man.

My heart leapt. That's a cliché, but it really did leap as I watched him approach, his arms and legs moving in a slow, sure rhythm as he skied.

Waving and shouting inanely, I ran to meet him. "Hulloa there! Over here!"

A stocky figure in a sheepskin coat, he wore huge fur mittens, canvas boots, a shapeless fur cap. Beneath it I saw a frost-crusted beard and a walrus moustache; bristling brows and small bright eyes.

I was grinning like a madman, but I couldn't stop. "Trapper Bjørvik, I presume? *Welcome!* You are most, most welcome!"

My visitor leaned on his ski poles in a haze of frosty breath. "*Ja*," he said, drawing off one mitten and taking my hand in a crushing grip. "Bjørvik."

Later

....

I made a complete fool of myself.

I gushed, I babbled, I pawed. He was good enough not to mind, or at least not to show it. With the unpretentious formality that's so endearing in Scandinavians, he presented me with his "visiting gift": a sack of reindeer hearts, ptarmigan livers and other choice cuts, which — with his rucksack, sleeping bag and rifle — he'd carried on his back the twenty miles from his cabin.

He didn't say why he'd come, or how long he meant to stay, and I didn't ask. Eriksson once told me that in Spitsbergen you tend not to ask, you simply assume that your guest will stay at least a week, and that his purpose is simply to visit.

"I know I'm talking too much," I blurted out as we took off our things in the porch, "but I've been alone for nearly three weeks." I flushed. It occurred to me that Bjørvik must have been on his own for months.

"*Ja*," he grunted, pulling off his boots. "Is good to visit."

His boots were "trapper's boots": a double thickness of canvas with a rubber sole, worn over two pairs of socks, and stuffed with straw. He wore the blue drill overalls of a sealer, with a heavy sweater of undyed wool

152

that smelt powerfully of sheep. Belatedly, I realised he was poor.

As flustered as a young hostess giving her first dinner, I sat him down, then bustled about lighting lamps, getting the stove going, making coffee. He planted his red hands on his knees and stared about him.

I found music on the wireless. I put together an enormous meal: tinned stewed veal and spinach, eggs, bacon, cheese, oatcakes, tinned cherries with condensed milk, peanut brittle, and everything else I could think of. To hell with my ration plan. This man had skied twenty miles to see me.

We ate in bashful silence. At least, I was abashed, as my conversational sallies had met with monosyllables. But Bjørvik told me later that he was simply absorbed in listening to Ivor Novello on the wireless. He doesn't own a radio, and it's been two years since he heard music.

After we'd eaten, I offered whisky and tobacco. Declining the whisky with grave dignity, he filled his pipe. By this time I'd stopped worrying about the monosyllables. I've never enjoyed a smoke as much as I did then.

Ivor Novello gave way to the news programme, and I lowered the volume.

"Is good," said Bjørvik with his slow nod.

Resisting the temptation to nod back, lest he mistake it for mimicry, I agreed that it was good, very good; although I didn't know if he meant the food, music, tobacco or me.

I said, "You know, in England I used to prefer being on my own. Now I think the best thing in life is having a visitor."

Beneath his brows, his eyes glinted. Slapping his knee, he barked a laugh. "*Ja!* Is good!"

I'm writing this in my bunk. Bjørvik is in Algie's, the bottom one nearest the window. He's snoring softly: a wondrous sound.

I'm not alone any more.

To see the cabin windows aglow when I come in. To feel the warmth of a well-stoked stove. And when I'm inside, to hear his tread on the boardwalk, his whistling as he chops wood and fetches ice from the stream. Yesterday feels like a million years ago.

Ja. Is good.

12th November

Two days have flown by. Yesterday I had a transmission from Algie. He said all's fine, but it'll be "a few days" before they set off. I can cope with that now because I'm not alone. No one could have a better, kinder, easier house guest. In many ways, he reminds me of Eriksson. The same rugged face, which at times undergoes a seismic shift as an earthquake of laughter rumbles to the surface. The same half-humorous, half-admiring respect for young English "yentlemen" with their passion for the weather. The same avuncular protectiveness: as if I were a talented but ignorant nephew who must be watched lest he blunder into trouble. I call him "Mister Bjørvik" and he calls me "Mister Yack".

In deference to his ways, we eat our main meal at two. After that we play cards or listen to the wireless — but never at the same time, as he thinks that's disrespectful to the BBC. At eight we eat a simple supper of eggs and bacon, and at half past nine he bids me good night and turns in, while I sit up, relishing the security.

He's used to plain food, mostly seal and reindeer (he calls it all "beef"); flour bannocks, blubber, dried apricots, and gallons of coffee. It delights me to treat him to tinned mutton and pork, Australian fruit salad, tinned vegetables, Digestive biscuits and chocolate. Yesterday he shot a reindeer (he calmly ignores their protected status) and we had huge, succulent steaks and blood pancakes — which are delicious; you don't taste the blood. We also ate the slippery marrow from the hind legs, which was delicious too, but had me making frequent trips to the outhouse, much to Bjørvik's amusement.

My favourite time is after supper. I read and smoke, and he smokes and carves: a pair of clogs for the cold weather to come, an antler sheath for his knife. He's devouring Algie's crime novels, and is particularly fond of Edgar Wallace.

Several times an hour, I go to the window and check the sky for clouds. I know it's silly, but I can't help myself. I resent the least haze obscuring the moon. And it happens so suddenly: one moment you're looking at that bright, pure disc; the next it's gone, swallowed by

155

inky darkness. I thought Bjørvik would laugh at my anxiety, but he doesn't even smile. I get the sense that he understands exactly why I need the light.

I haven't mentioned the haunting, and he hasn't spoken of it, but I'm sure that he knows. He tells me he's been hunting on this part of the coast for years. He knows. Once, when I asked if he's ever experienced *rar*, he gave me a wary look and said he's never had any "trouble" on *his* stretch of the coast. And this evening when I said I prefer this wind we're having to "the dead stillness", he said, "*Ja*. The stillness. When you hear yourself blink. Is terrible." Later he asked about the bear post, and when I told him I'd cut it down, he frowned.

That was my chance. I should have said something. Why didn't I?

Because I don't *want* to. Because I'm afraid that if I talk of it, I might somehow invoke it. Back in August, at "first dark", Eriksson asked if I'd spoken to it. I understand now why he thought that was important. For the same reason, I don't want to mention it to Bjørvik; because I feel that if I did, I'd be inviting it in.

Besides, with any luck I won't need to. If all goes well and the sea stays clear, Gus and Algie will be back before Bjørvik leaves.

14th November

A storm blew up after I wrote that: a north wind from the Pole. It's over now, but this morning the sky was so overcast that I couldn't see the moon, and the bay was full of ice.

I was horrified. The sea was gone. In its place were huge chaotic slabs and tilting pinnacles, like some fantastic frozen city. I couldn't believe it. The pack ice isn't supposed to arrive until after New Year.

When I said so to Bjørvik, he barked a laugh. "*Nej, nej*, Mister Yack, this is not pack ice! That come in *Januar*, and you will know it, you will see the *islyning*, the ice blink, when it throw the light in the sky. This is just drift ice from the storm. Very dangery, you stay off it, Mister Yack. But don't worry, soon the wind change and the ice it clear."

He was right, of course. The wind has changed, and already it's blowing the ice out to sea.

I wish I knew as much as Bjørvik. Maybe then I'd be able to cope with this place.

He leads a life of unimaginable solitude. His main cabin is on Wijdefjord, but he's built four smaller ones a few days' walk away, with scores of fox traps and self-shooting bear traps in between. He baits his fox traps with seabird heads, his bear traps with seal blubber, and checks them every fortnight. He wouldn't have had time to visit me if it hadn't been for the storm. It brought the deep snow, and foxes avoid that, as they fear becoming trapped in drifts, and eaten by bears.

He says that overhunting has made the catch worse than it used to be. Last winter he only caught twelve foxes and two bears; although he got a decent price for the furs, and a chemist in Tromsø gave him twenty-four krøner for the bears' gall bladders, which are a cure for rheumatism.

I find it odd that he can speak of those awe-inspiring bears and beautiful little foxes as if they were no more than animated furs; and yet he tamed an orphaned cub as a *husrev* (a "house fox"), and grieved when it sickened and died. I suppose he's too poor to be sentimental about animals. That's a privilege only the middle classes can afford. I suspect he deplores my lavishing butterscotch on Isaak, although he's too polite to show it. And certainly he disapproves of the dogs running wild. (To placate him I've reverted to staking them by "day" and shutting them up at night, which they hate.)

I wish I knew why he always hunts alone, but he hasn't said, and I won't ask. Once, though, he let slip that when he was young, he wasn't "God's best disciple". And from other things, I gather that there are aspects of his past which he regrets.

The sky is clear again and the moon is back — although I'm alarmed to see how much it's waned. It changes all the time. Sometimes it's pale-gold, sometimes blue-white. Sometimes it's in a greyish halo, edged faintly with red.

But in fact it's not any of those colours, it's some moon colour I can't describe. Or perhaps it's no colour at all; perhaps the light isn't strong enough to allow my eyes to see in colour, so that what I'm seeing is the world in black and white, as Isaak sees it.

And why do I even try to describe the colours? Is it the human compulsion to name things, to assert control? Perhaps the same compulsion drives our meteorology: all that observing, measuring, recording. Trying to render bearable this vast, silent land.

And is that, too, why I've been writing this journal? To set down everything clearly, make sense of it? If it can be described, it can be understood. If it can be understood, it need not be feared.

I say "to set down everything", but of course, I've been selective. And having flicked through these pages, I'm surprised at what I've chosen to put in. Why did I begin with that corpse being pulled from the Thames? And why mention that black-faced polar bear guarding its kill?

No, it's wrong to say that I'm *surprised* at my selection. I'm alarmed. I don't like the pattern I'm making.

And again, why write at all?

Am I trying to make sense of what I've experienced, or am I trying to push it into the past, to stop it bleeding into the present?

If I was a different kind of man, I might be doing this to leave a record behind as a warning to others, in case something happens to me. But I'm not unselfish enough for that. I don't care what happens after I'm dead. (Although I do note the contradiction: on the one hand, I don't believe that anything of myself will survive death, while on the other, I know that Gruhuken is haunted.)

So if it isn't that, then what? Am I trying to perform some kind of exorcism? Can you do that by writing things down?

After the War, Father suffered the most dreadful nightmares. In fact we all suffered, as his screams used to wake the whole house. One night, matters came to a head (almost literally). While sleepwalking, Father grabbed his service revolver from under his pillow and shot a German officer who — he told us afterwards — he distinctly saw standing at the foot of the bed. The bullet passed clean through the bedroom wall and six inches over my head as I lay asleep in the next room. The following day, Mother took the gun and "disposed of it" (I've no idea how), and made Father see a nerve doctor. The doctor told him to write an account of his experiences in the trenches — "to exorcise his demons". Of course he didn't. And the nightmares didn't last. He was already ill with the TB which killed him two months later.

But is that, I wonder, what I'm trying to do now? Exorcise my demons?

Again, there's an inconsistency. I want to exorcise the haunting by writing about it, but I don't want to mention it out loud, for fear of invoking it.

And how *can* I exorcise it, when I don't know what it is?

Later
....

That was a digression, but it did help clarify my thoughts.

I know that Gruhuken is haunted. I know this. Some angry spirit walks this place. It is not an echo. It has intent. It wishes me ill.

160

And I don't know how to appease it, or exorcise it, because I don't know who — what — it is. Or what it wants.

Bjørvik knows something. I'm sure of it. I have to make him tell me. And I can't put it off any longer. Soon he'll leave. He's been away nearly a week; he has to check his traps.

I've thought about going with him. But we couldn't take the dogs; they'd scare away the foxes and ruin his livelihood. And I can't leave them, I can't shoot them, I can't let the expedition fail. Same old arguments. Besides, it's only a matter of days before Gus and Algie get back.

I can't put it off any longer. I have to talk to Bjørvik.

He has to tell me what he knows.

CHAPTER
FOURTEEN

16th November
....

Bjørvik is leaving tomorrow. He asked me to go with him.

It was after supper; we were on our second mugs of coffee. "Mister Yack. When I go, you come too, *ja?* You bring the dogs. You stay with me."

It touched me deeply that he offered to take the dogs as well, but I also found it alarming. What danger does he think I'm in that he'd risk his livelihood to help me?

For one crazy moment, I nearly said yes. But I can't do that to him. And I can't break faith with Algie and Gus. All right, to hell with Algie, I can't break faith with Gus. *JACK YOU'RE AMAZING! EXPEDITION SCUPPERED WITHOUT YOU!* That's what it comes down to.

I keep picturing what it'll be like when he gets back. His blue eyes shining with gratitude and admiration. *You did it, Jack. I didn't think anyone could, but you pulled it off!*

That's ridiculous, I know, and writing it makes me cringe, but that doesn't stop me playing it over and over in my head.

Which is why, when Bjørvik asked me to go with him, I said no.

As I was trying to explain my reasons, it suddenly occurred to me that this was the third time I've refused an offer to leave Gruhuken. First Eriksson, then Gus, now Bjørvik. There's a horrible symmetry to that. In fairy tales, don't things always come in threes? And in the Bible? Three times before the cock crows . . . It's as if I've been fated to be here on my own since the beginning.

After I'd finished, Bjørvik said simply, "But Mister Yack. Your friends. How long till they come?"

"Not long. They're setting out soon, they'll be here in three days at the most. They're wiring me tomorrow morning to finalise things."

He didn't reply.

I fetched the coffee pot and refilled our mugs. I spilt some on the table. I sat down and met his eyes. I said, "Gruhuken is haunted."

His gaze never left my face. "*Ja.*"

Isn't talking about things supposed to make them better? Well it didn't. I felt as if I'd opened the window and let something in.

"Tell me," I said. "Tell me what haunts this place."

He took a pull at his coffee and set down his mug. "Is not good to talk of this."

"But we must."

"Mister Yack. There are things in the world we don't understand. Is best to leave it like this."

"Mister Bjørvik. Please. I have to know."

He was silent for a long time, staring into the stove's red heart. "Nobody knew his name," he said. "A trapper. Men called him bad names. He never seemed to hear."

I stared at him. "You — knew him?"

"Nobody knew him. Once when I was young, I saw him. In Longyearbyen, twenty-six, twenty-seven year ago." He grimaced. "When he was alive."

I swallowed. "So this was — 1910, or thereabouts. Before the War."

"*Ja*. It all happen before the War."

What he told me then came out in fits and starts, with long silences in between. He hated telling me, but I was relentless. Nobody knew where the trapper had come from. The wilds of north Norway. Somewhere poor. He worked his way to Spitsbergen on a whaling ship. He was ugly, and he had that abject manner which brings out the worst in people, particularly men. They gave him the filthiest, most degrading tasks. That was all it took: nothing more than an abject manner and ill-favoured looks. Bjørvik called him something in Norwegian; I think it means God-forgotten. One of life's rejects.

At Longyearbyen he tried to get a place in the mines, but he wasn't strong enough, so they wouldn't take him. He tried selling fossils to tourists, but his appearence affronted them. Somehow he got work on a sealer, and found his way to an isolated bay in the north. There he built a driftwood hut and took to fur trapping.

For a few years he lived there on his own. Every summer, he would turn up in Longyearbyen to sell his skins and pick up supplies. He couldn't read and he'd

164

never handled money, so people cheated him. After a few days he was gone again, back to the one place where no one set the dogs on him and called him names.

Gruhuken.

A mining syndicate took it from him. In this whole vast wilderness they had to have this one lonely bay. They'd found coal here. They staked their claim and threw him out.

"I don't understand," I said. "We found their claim sign. The — Edinburgh Prospecting Company, something like that, but it was dated 1905. Wasn't that *before* he got here?"

"*Ja*, for sure. But Mister Yack, those signs, they say what they want."

"You mean — they backdated their claim? Wasn't that illegal?"

He snorted. "This was no-man's-land! No law! They do what they like!"

"So although he was here first . . ."

"He was one, they were many. They throw him out."

"And then?"

He chewed his moustache. "He came back . . . They say they sent him on his way. They say they never saw him again."

"'They say'. You mean it wasn't like that?"

His gaze slid to the fire. "I don't know. After that, nobody saw him. Alive."

"But — you know something. Don't you?"

He shifted uncomfortably. "When miners have money, Mister Yack, they drink. When they drink, they talk. In those days, I drink too. One night I am in the bar in Longyear . . ." He broke off.

"And they were there? The miners from Gruhuken?"

". . . One only. By then the others were dead."

"And this miner, he told you what happened?"

"No."

"But he talked and you overheard?"

He glared at me. "He was drinking himself to death. He made no sense."

"But you guessed. What did they do to him, the trapper of Gruhuken?"

Suddenly he sprang to his feet, overturning his chair. "As God is my witness," he bellowed, "I *don't know!*"

A shocked silence.

Slowly, Bjørvik righted his chair, and sat down, and scowled at the floor.

I got up and walked to the window, then returned to my seat. "I'm sorry. But — even if you don't *know*, I think you guessed something. Tell me what you think happened."

He rubbed a hand over his face. "I think — I think when he came back — they were angry. I think at first they want just to beat him. Then it turn into something else." He swallowed. "Men like that — when they know they won't be found out — they will do anything."

Glancing down, I saw that my hands were clenched. I thought of the blotchy stains on the bear post. I felt sick.

After that, there wasn't much to tell. The mine limped on for another year, but it was dogged by misfortune. A cable severed a man's leg and he bled to

166

death. A boat overturned, drowning two men within sight of the shore. Finally, a rockslide destroyed the cabins, and the surviving miners left. The following year, the prospecting company decided that the deposit wasn't rich enough after all, and abandoned the mine.

Gruhuken stood deserted. It swiftly gained a bad reputation. People who camped here met with accidents. Fire. Drowning. A Swedish trapper shot his companion and then himself. The note on the body said he'd done it to escape the *gengånger* — "the one who walks again".

There Bjørvik's account ended. But I know the rest of the story. For over two decades, Gruhuken remained deserted. Then in 1935, topographers from Oxford University surveyed this stretch of coast and mentioned this bay as a likely site for future expeditions. Shortly afterwards, Gus Balfour read their report and put Gruhuken at the top of his list.

The lamp had burned out. I refilled it and replaced it on the table. The smell of paraffin made me sick.

Bjørvik sat with his hands on his knees, staring at the floor.

I'd intended to tell him what I've experienced here, but I couldn't bring myself to do it. And he didn't want to know.

I asked if he'd ever been to Gruhuken before now, and he said no, he's never hunted within ten miles of the bay. I asked if he'd experienced anything untoward while he's been here. He said his dreams have been "bad". Only his dreams? I envy him that.

Again I went to the window. I couldn't see the moon. A wind was blowing from the east, sending fingers of snow across the shore. I turned back to Bjørvik. "What does it want?"

He spread his hands.

I understood.

It wants Gruhuken.

And I'm in the way.

17th November

I should have gone with him.

But I was so sure that Gus and Algie would be back in a day or so. Convinced that I could hold out until then.

My hands are sweating. My fingers keep slipping on the pen. Why didn't I go with him?

He left nearly three hours ago, just after breakfast. Although the moon is in its last quarter, the Northern Lights were bright, and he said he'd have plenty of light for skiing. He didn't repeat his offer to take me in, and I knew that since we'd spoken of the haunting, he couldn't wait to leave. I was right about that; talking has brought it closer.

I wanted him to give me some wise advice, or a talisman for repelling ghosts, as garlic is supposed to repel vampires. Even a Bible would have been a comfort. I don't believe in God, but I would've regarded it as a superior kind of amulet. I told him this — not about the amulet, but about the Bible; I tried to make a joke of it — but he shook his head. A Bible wouldn't help.

I gave him a parting gift: as much bacon as he can carry, a packet of our best Virginia tobacco, and the four Edgar Wallaces he hasn't yet read. He was pleased. So at least I got that right.

The last thing he said before he left was to be sure and keep the dogs close.

At first I didn't feel too bad about being on my own again. Then an hour later I "spoke" to Algie.

I'd expected it to be Gus. I'd been looking forward to it. But it turns out that Gus has had some kind of "setback". Algie swears he's not in danger, and I don't think he'd lie about that. But it means they can't set out yet. *SORRY JACK A WEEK TILL WE CAN LEAVE SORRY STOP*

I was in shock. I couldn't take it in. Numbly, I sent back an acknowledgement. *THAT'S OK STOP TELL GUS GET BETTER SOON STOP*

OK? How is it OK? A week till they leave means maybe nine days before they get here. That's nearly December. How can I hope that the coast will be clear of ice? I could be stuck here till spring. I'll never make it.

When I got the transmission, I thought about going after Bjørvik. To hell with everything, just strap on your skis and get out of here.

But by then he'd had two hours' start on me. And I don't know where his camp is. It isn't on the map. All I know is that it's somewhere on the far side of Wijdefjord, which is vast.

169

I even thought of tracking him. But the wind has obliterated his trail.

My wristwatch has stopped, but according to Gus' alarm clock, it's eleven in the "morning". Another hour till I have to go outside and do the readings.

Yes, we're back to that again. Back to bolstering your courage with whisky and cigarettes. Back to bribing the dogs with sweets to keep them with you. Back to watching the sky for the least trace of cloud.

I keep wondering what they did to him, the trapper of Gruhuken. I think of that miner I saw at Longyearbyen. *Men like that — when they know they won't be found out — they will do anything.*

I remember the malevolence of that figure in front of the cabin. The endless black inhuman rage.

How can I hold out for another week?

Later

....

I had a massive drink and a stiff talk with myself, and I feel a little steadier.

What you've got to remember, Jack, is that it can't *do* anything to you. That's what I keep coming back to. That's why I still cling to the hope that I *can* hang on here until the others arrive.

Because what haunts this place is merely *spirit*. It is not *matter*. Not as I am matter, not as this pen and notebook and table are matter.

It can't hurt me. All it can do is frighten.

170

CHAPTER
FIFTEEN

18th November

....

I knew things would change, but I didn't expect it to happen so quickly, and I never thought it would involve the dogs.

While Bjørvik was here, I couldn't really imagine what it would be like when he left. A day later and it's as if his visit never took place. The moon has waned. It's just a slit in the sky. The dark is back.

Once, I thought fear of the dark was the oldest fear of all. Maybe I was wrong. Maybe it's not the dark that people fear, but what comes in the dark. What exists in it.

I'm prevaricating. The dogs.

Yesterday after Bjørvik left, I made a titanic effort to absorb the shock about Gus and Algie. I mustered my courage and did my work. I prepared food and forced it down.

As I went about my duties, I experienced nothing untoward. No presence. No dread. Only a shrinking inside me: the apprehension of what might come.

By half past six I'd fed the dogs and was facing my first evening alone. I wasn't hungry, and although I was tired, I knew I wouldn't sleep, so I did what I've never done before and won't do again: I knocked myself out with morphine.

I slept for twelve hours, and woke ten minutes before the 7a.m. readings. I made it by a whisker.

I was on the bicycle generator, about to start transmitting, when I remembered I hadn't let out the dogs — or rather, they reminded me with indignant complaints from the doghouse. As I was already late for Bear Island, I shouted to them to wait, and set to work. At one point I think I was aware that their howls became louder, then abruptly ceased. Or maybe that's my imagination, adding details in retrospect. When I got outside, the doghouse door was open and they were gone.

I waved my lantern. "Isaak! Kiawak! Upik! Jens! Eli! Svarten! Pakomi! Anadark! *Isaak!*"

Nothing.

It's not like them. They've never strayed, not even into the next bay. Huskies don't. At least, ours don't. And they always come when I call, as they know that I mean food.

That was twelve hours ago.

How did they get out? What were they trying to escape? What happened to them?

I've left food for them in front of the cabin, and wedged open the doghouse door, with more food inside. I know that risks attracting bears, but I don't care. I'll do anything to get them back.

And they will come back, won't they, when they're hungry? And since they're always hungry, they'll come back soon.

But what if they don't?

172

....

Two days since Bjørvik left. One since the dogs disappeared.

I walk bent over, as if there were a tumour in my gut. I miss the dogs. Without them, there's nothing between me and what haunts this place.

It can come at any time. It can stay away for days, as it did when Bjørvik was here. But always I sense it waiting. That's the worst of it. Not knowing when it will come. Only that it will.

A few years ago, I read a speech in the paper by the American President; he said, *The only thing we have to fear is fear itself.* He doesn't know. He doesn't know.

I've tried to pity the trapper of Gruhuken. He had a miserable life and a terrible death. But I can't. All I feel is dread.

And knowing who he was doesn't help me, because I can't do anything to appease him. It doesn't matter that I'm innocent. It isn't only the guilty who suffer.

Besides, I *am* guilty. Because I'm here.

20th November
....

ISAAK IS BACK!

I found him huddled against the door when I returned from the noon readings. He was in a terrible state, soaking wet and shaking with fright. I fell to my knees and flung my arms about him, "Isaak, Isaak!"

173

And still that convulsive shivering, panting with terror, his black lips drawn back, and a wildness in his eyes that I'd never seen before.

Where have you been? I wanted to ask. *Tell me what you saw.*

When I opened the door he was through it in a flash, scrabbling to get into the hall. Then he shot under my bunk and refused to come out.

All entreaties failed, but at last a chunk of butterscotch succeeded. I towelled him down and fed him a tin of pemmican, and gradually the shaking eased and he became more like himself. His fur fluffed up in the heat of the stove, his eyes lost their wildness. But when I rose to hang up the towel, he followed me anxiously, keeping so close to my heels that I nearly fell over.

"Don't worry, Isaak," I told him. "From now on you're staying in here with me. No more doghouse for you, my lad. You're safe."

He watched my face, his ears twitching as he listened.

It's amazing how reassuring it is to have someone to soothe. It makes you so much braver and more resourceful. I suppose that's how parents feel. You've got to say strong for the children.

"But the thing is," I went on, "if I left you free to roam around in here, you'd eat everything in sight. So I'm afraid I'm going to have to tie you up."

To stop him chewing the rope, I soaked it in paraffin. Then I tied one end to his harness and the other to the most immovable thing in the cabin: my bunk.

Of course it didn't work. When I was out of sight in the main room he set up a heart-rending yowl. And it turns out that he quite likes paraffin: he dispatched the rope in five minutes. So instead I dog-proofed the cabin as best I could, moving everything remotely chewable to the upper bunks and shelves. Then I scattered a few sticks of driftwood as decoys and set him free.

Ignoring the driftwood, he burnt his nose on the stove, then rushed about, sniffing and lifting his leg whenever I couldn't stop him. Soon he began to pant alarmingly, and I realised he was hot. I gave him a bowl of water. He lapped desultorily and continued to pant. I fetched a big bowl of snow. Better. He snapped it up and the panting lessened. After that he found my reindeer hides, which I'd forgotten to move off my bunk, and settled down to eat them.

I'd been so busy that I'd missed the five o'clock readings, and had to wire an excuse to Bear Island. I didn't care. It's wonderful having Isaak with me. To hear the click of his claws on the floor. To feel his cold nose nudging my palm. He's not house-trained — he's never *been* in a house — so I have to watch him constantly, and that's exactly what I need. Just now he started to squat, so I grabbed him by the harness and dragged him outside. I stood with my back to the door, like a suburban householder trying to persuade Fido to do his business. I felt no hint of the presence. Nor did Isaak show any signs of fear. The food I'd set out for the dogs was still there in the snow, but to my surprise, he ignored it. Instead, when he'd done what he needed, he trotted off a few paces and stood facing seawards, with the wind at his back. Then he lifted his muzzle and howled. I felt the hairs rise on the nape of my neck. Such loneliness. Such grief.

It didn't sound as if he was calling his pack. It sounded as if he knows they're never coming back.

21st November
....

He still howls for his pack, but he's becoming accustomed to being inside, and I no longer have to watch him all the time.

Nor do I need to worry about my wirelesses, because he never goes near that end of the cabin. He becomes agitated when I'm working there. Wise dog. I wish I could do as he does, and stay away.

This morning, I nearly missed my talk with Gus because of Isaak. I'd switched on the Eddystone, but Isaak was about to squat, so I'd taken him out, and when we got back inside, the lights were flickering.

I rushed to put on the head-phones; I didn't want to miss a single one of those disembodied dits and dahs which are Gus' words coming through the ether.

JACK WHERE ARE YOU? ARE YOU OK? JACK!

That he'd used an expression like "OK" made me smile. It reminded me of one of our first conversations on board the *Isbjørn*, when I'd said "OK" and he'd said "grand", and I'd been so touchy. So I couldn't resist using his own word in reply. *I'M GRAND STOP HOW ARE YOU?*

176

Being Gus, he got it at once. *OH HA HA BUT I WAS WORRIED!*

DOGS GONE BUT ISAAK HERE STOP

WHAT? WHAT?

I told him about the dogs, and Isaak coming back. I explained that Bjørvik had left, although I didn't mention that he'd asked me to go with him and I'd refused. Gus' anxiety crackled through the wires, and I basked in it. I was like Isaak: it didn't matter what Gus said, it was the fact that he said it which counted. The fact that he cares enough to worry. *JACK YOU ARE SO BRAVE! EXPEDITION OWES ALL TO YOU!*

Yes it bloody well does, I thought. But because it was Gus, I flushed with pleasure.

When he'd gone, I stared at his words on the page. I couldn't bear to put them in the stove, so I slipped them inside this journal.

I've never felt this way about anyone. I suppose you'd call it hero worship. Or maybe I cling to him because I'm so frightened. All I know is that if he was here now, I could bear anything.

The silence after the noisy transmission was awful. The cabin looked smoke-stained and dirty. Everywhere I turned I saw Gus' possessions. His microscope, his books. Piles of his clothes on the upper bunks, like bodies.

And around the table, five chairs. Five. A convocation of ghosts.

Then I spotted some scraps of reindeer hide underneath, which Isaak had missed. I got down on hands and knees to pick them up, and he padded over to investigate, and I felt better.

I don't know what I'd do without him. I love the way he slumps down with a *humph*, and thumps his tail at my approach. I love it when he lies on his belly with his muzzle between his paws, and twitches his eyebrows to follow my every move. I love the leathery smell of his pads, and the croaky ror-ror-ror noises he makes when he's talking to me. His eyes are extraordinary. They're not ice blue as I used to think, but *warm*: the light, clear blue of a summer morning. I know that's ridiculously over the top, but it's true.

As I write, he's under the table, leaning against my calf. I reach down and sink my fingers into his fur. I feel the heat of his flank and his muscled ribs; the rapid beat of his heart.

I keep breaking off to talk to him. "We won't be parted again, I promise. When all this is over, you're coming home with me. To England, Isaak, that's where I live. I don't care how much it costs or how long it takes. People do keep huskies in England; Gus knows a family in Berkshire, they've got three. I'll get a job in the country. You'll like it there. And you'll love chasing rabbits. You've never seen a rabbit, but you'll know at once that it's got to be chased. You'll be good at it, too. And I'll find you a mate, and you'll father puppies. You can start your own pack."

Isaak sits with his muzzle on my thigh, gazing up at me with his extraordinary eyes.

178

The south wind is still blowing, breaking up the last of the ice. I can see the black water in the bay. I hold on to that. The bay is still open. They can still get back.

Somewhere on the outside of the cabin, a corner of tarpaper is flapping. A while ago I ventured out and tried to find it, but I couldn't. And I didn't try for very long.

Soon after I got back inside, Isaak became restless. Not playful or hungry or wanting to go out, not looking for a place to squat. He moved about, panting, but ignoring the bowl of snow in the bunkroom. His ears were back and his head was low. His eyes were glassy. He was afraid.

"Isaak?"

He ignored me.

I grabbed a lantern and a torch and stood in the middle of the room.

Isaak stopped a few feet from the north window. His hackles rose.

I held my breath, listening. My eyes darted from window to window.

Suddenly, Isaak shook himself. Then he turned to me and faintly wagged his tail.

I breathed out.

After that I couldn't face going outside, so I skipped the five o'clock readings and wired another excuse to Bear Island. I feel bad about that. I don't like to think that the rot is setting in. Tomorrow I'll get back to my routine.

My routine. I cling to it. It's all I've got. But I'm beginning to worry about time — that is, about being able to keep track of it. My wristwatch still won't work, and today I discovered that the Stevenson's self-timer has broken. This means that all I've got left to mark the time is Gus' alarm clock. Tomorrow when I go outside, I'll take it with me in my pocket, wrapped in a muffler to protect it from the cold. For now, it sits on the table in the main room.

It's the only thing I've got left to tell me that the days are going by. There's no longer any twilight at midday, and the moon has dwindled to a lightless sliver. Tomorrow it will be gone.

Tomorrow it's the dark of the moon.

CHAPTER
SIXTEEN

22nd November
....

Last night I learned what Bjørvik couldn't tell me. I learned what happened to the trapper of Gruhuken.

I sat up late, writing and talking to Isaak. Around eleven, I let him out, and when he came back inside I put a bowl of snow for him in the bunkroom and we settled down to sleep.

Cold outside, twenty-five below. Inside, our breath crusted the bunkroom walls with hoar frost. I couldn't get warm. I coaxed Isaak on to the bunk, but he soon jumped down. He curled up on the floor, but not for long. I couldn't tell if he'd caught the restlessness from me, or if he was sensing something.

Despite two sleeping bags and the remaining reindeer hides, I couldn't stop shivering. Eventually I went into the hall and unearthed our portable paraffin stove from beneath the dog harnesses, and set it up in the bunkroom. Because of Isaak, this meant dragging the packing cases from the opposite wall and positioning the stove on top, where he couldn't knock it down.

Much better.

I dream I'm in a rowing boat with Gus. The swell rocks us gently. It's wonderfully peaceful. Together we peer over the side and watch the kelp swaying in the clear water.

The boat tilts slightly backwards, and I glance over my shoulder. A hand has risen from the sea to grasp the gunwale. I'm not frightened, merely determined. I won't let that thing haul itself out.

I'm holding a large knife, and with a grimace of distaste I start sawing at the fingers. My blade snags in the flesh. I yank it free. I keep trying. It's like cutting up a chicken when you've missed the joint and have to saw through the bone. I'm faintly disgusted, but I also find it satisfying.

The dream shifts. Now I'm in the sea, deep down in blackness. Again I'm not frightened, only disgusted. A drowned thing is clasping me in its arms. Together we roll in the slippery kelp. I can't see its face, but I feel its cheek pressed against mine, cold and soft as mouldering leather.

Now I'm tied to the bear post. Now I'm afraid. I can't see. I can't speak. I have no tongue. I smell paraffin. I hear the crackle of flames. I know that someone nearby is holding a torch.

Now I hear the clink of metal dragged over rocks. Dread squeezes my heart. It's coming closer. I can't get away. I'm bound hand and foot. Clink. Clink. Closer. The terror is overwhelming. It's coming for me. I can't move I can't *move* . . .

With a cry I woke up.

Isaak nosed my face, his whiskers brushing my cheek. I lay gasping and shuddering, my heart pounding so hard that it hurt.

182

I was cold. My sleeping bag was damp. Putting out a hand, I felt the wall. Wet. It took me a moment to realise what had happened. The stove had melted the hoar frost.

The dream was still with me. I knew that the terror I had felt had not been my own. I thought of the blotchy stains on the bear post. The sound of metal dragged over rocks.

That's when I remembered what I'd forgotten before: the rusty relics which we found when we first came to Gruhuken. We buried them to make the place safe for the dogs. Wire. Gaffs. Knives. Big, rusty knives: the sort that you use once you've gaffed your seal and dragged it ashore.

Flensing knives.

I didn't make it to the slop pail. I vomited in the doorway till my belly ached.

Isaak padded after me and lapped up the sick.

Shaky as an old man, I hobbled to the kitchen. I filled Isaak's bowl and set it down. I watched him sniff it. I scooped water into a mug and tried to drink. My teeth were chattering. I couldn't swallow. I kept seeing flashes from the dream.

Flensing knives.

When men know they won't be found out, they will do anything.

When I was eight, I saw some older boys torture a dog. At first they only kicked it. Then one of them took out his penknife and slit its eyes. I remember watching it stagger down the street. I was desperate for its suffering to end; please please let it be run over. But the creature blundered across the road and round the corner, and when I got there it was gone. For weeks I prayed that it had died quickly. But young as I was, I suspected that a God who allows such cruelty wouldn't have cared about bringing it to an end.

I don't want to think about what they did to the trapper of Gruhuken. I can still hear the clink of metal as they dragged the gaffs over the stones; as they threw down the knives and got to work.

And after they'd finished with the knives, that's when the paraffin came in, and the torches. I wish I could believe that he was dead by then, but I don't think he was.

I don't want this in my head. I wish I could scour my mind clean.

It's two in the morning but I dread going back to sleep. If the dream came again . . .

So instead, I'm going to deal with this hoar frost. Bjørvik told me a trick about that. You nail blankets to the walls and ceiling, and somehow that stops it collecting.

There. I've done it. I've lined the bunkroom with blankets. Having to concentrate on hammering in the nails has steadied me a bit.

Even though it's just occurred to me that what I've created is a padded cell.

Later
....

I thought it wanted me gone, but now I know better.

I must have fallen asleep, because I woke huddled in my bunk. The window was a faint charcoal oblong in

184

the dark. Isaak stood in the middle of the room. His hackles were up, his ears flat back.

Outside, near my head, a step on the boardwalk. A heavy, wet, irregular tread.

Sweat chilled my skin. I lay frozen, listening to the footsteps pass slowly down the boardwalk towards the front of the cabin. I groped in the bedclothes for my torch. Isaak came and leaned, shivering, against my bunk. I found my torch but didn't switch it on. I watched something dark move past the bunkroom window.

Clutching my torch like a talisman, I swung my legs over the side of the bunk. I stumbled into the main room. Isaak followed.

I dreaded to hear the steps halt at the porch, but they continued past as if it didn't exist. Feeling my way, I shuffled towards the north window. Nothing. I turned to the west window. There. Half seen at the edge. Something dark.

The steps on the boardwalk ceased.

I waited. Isaak stood behind me, panting with fear. My breath smoked. I began to shiver. Still I waited.

At last I couldn't stand it any longer, and went and huddled in my sleeping bag. Isaak crawled under my bunk.

I listened for an hour. It didn't come back.

For Isaak's sake, I decided to create a semblance of normality. I got up and pulled on some clothes, and lit the stove in the main room, and the lamps, and made the cabin as bright and warm as I could. I opened a tin of pemmican and emptied it on to one of the Royal

185

Doulton plates, and watched him gulp it down, rattling the plate across the floor as he licked it clean. To my surprise, I found that I was hungry too, so I scrambled four eider-duck eggs with half a pound of cheese. But once it was ready, I couldn't eat, so I gave it to Isaak.

By then he'd stopped trembling, although he stayed close at my heels. That's how it happened. I'd washed up and was putting things on the shelves when I turned and he couldn't get out of the way and I fell over. I crashed against the table and sent the alarm clock flying.

It broke. Something inside me broke, too.

"Stupid fucking *stupid* dog!" I shouted. "Stupid! Stupid!" I went on shouting, kicking and lashing out with my fists. He didn't try to get away; he cowered with his tail between his legs, not understanding what he'd done, only knowing that he was in the wrong because he's a dog and must take his beating.

Suddenly I realised what I was doing. I fell to my knees, I flung my arms around him and started to cry. Big jerky heaving sobs. I cried till I was exhausted. By this time, Isaak had extricated himself and retreated to a safe distance. I think my crying scared him more than anything.

Drained, I got up and went to the kitchen and washed my face. I didn't recognise myself in the shaving mirror. Who is this haggard, hairy man with the wild eyes and the grimy furrows down his cheeks?

That's when I knew I couldn't do this any more.

"All *right*," I said out loud. "You've won. Gruhuken is yours. I've had enough. I'm beaten. I'm getting out."

186

At this time in the morning, Ohlsen on Bear Island would be asleep, but there might be someone awake at the Longyearbyen wireless station. As soon as they received my Mayday, they'd wake Gus and Algie, who would wake Eriksson, and the *Isbjørn* would set off . . .

I'd forgotten about the hoar frost. It wasn't only in the bunkroom. Why should it be? And I'd done a good job of warming up the cabin. The Eddystone was beaded with moisture. So was the Gambrell and the Austin, and all my spare valves. Wet. Ruined. Useless.

That was a while ago — although of course I don't know exactly how long, because I haven't got a clock. I've mopped up as best I can, and hung the towels over the stove to dry. I don't know why I did this. Except that I'm the wireless operator, and I don't like leaving my equipment in a mess.

When Bear Island receives no transmissions for two days, they'll wire Longyearbyen to send help. Even if a ship can still get through, it'll take another two days. So that's four days at the earliest. Four days.

I try to believe that I can hold out till then. Come on, Jack, you've made it this far, just a little longer. But things are different now. There's no moon.

Four days. It'll be over by then.

I feel worst for Isaak. That makes me really angry. It's not his fault. He didn't ask to be brought here. It's not his *fault*.

My writing on the page is a deranged scrawl, but I know that I'm not mad. This is not a delusion. It's not some nerve storm brought on by solitude and dark. Something made Gus and Algie experience what they did. Something gave Bjørvik nightmares and opened the door of the doghouse and frightened the huskies away. Something terrified Isaak and trod the boardwalk outside.

Another thing just occurred to me as I was feeding logs to the stove. The trapper's hut. When we tore it down, we chopped it up and added the logs to the woodpile. By now, I must have brought some of them inside.

And those times in the storm, when the wind blew the smoke down the stovepipe and out into the room. That black smoke griming the walls, making me cough. The trapper's hut. I've breathed it in.

It's inside me.

Later

The stillness is back. The dead cold windless dark. *That's* the truth. The dark. We're the anomaly. Little flickering sparks on the crust of this spinning planet — and around it the dark.

Just now, I looked back to the start of this journal. I don't recognise the man who wrote it. Did he really spend a whole summer in endless light? Was he really so eager to reach Gruhuken? That strikes me as horrible.

Once he wrote that in the Arctic he would be able to see clearly, *right through to the heart of things*. Well you got what you wanted, didn't you, you poor fool? This is the truth: what walks here in the dark.

188

Some people think of death as a door into a better place. *For now we see through a glass, darkly; but then face to face . . .* What if it's not like that? What if there is no en*light*enment, and it's all just dark? What if the dead know no more than we?

Once when I was a boy I asked Father about ghosts, and he said, Jack, if they existed, don't you think Flanders would be full of them? And I said, do you mean they *don't* exist? And he said, maybe. Or maybe we just can't hear them.

To be conscious in eternal night. You would pray for oblivion. But there'd be no one to hear you.

Is that how it is for what haunts this place? Is that what it wants for me? Trapped here for ever in eternal night?

Later
....

I've just realised the significance of what I wrote about the doghouse. *Something opened the doghouse door.*

It can open doors.

It can get in.

I'm not going to write this journal any more. No point. I'm finished with it.

I suppose I should leave it here on the table in plain sight, so that if anyone comes, they'll find it and know what happened. But I'm not going to do that. This journal is *mine*: my words, and Gus' too, the notes of our wireless exchanges pasted in the back. I'm going to make sure that it stays with me always.

So here we are: the final page. Nothing left to write. Jack Miller's journal.

The End.

CHAPTER
SEVENTEEN

I've strapped my journal to my chest with a length of canvas webbing left over from the dogs' harnesses, and I'm wearing one of Gus' shirts on top. If by some miracle I get out of this alive, I'll tell him I mistook it for one of mine. If I die, I want something of his with me.

I'm sitting in my bunk in a mound of sleeping bags and reindeer hides. Five lamps are burning in the main room, and the stove is red hot (Isaak knows not to go near it). In here I've got the paraffin stove on the packing cases I pulled out from the wall, and a lamp on a chair beside me, and two torches against my thigh. It's warmer in the main room, but I prefer it in here. My padded cell. I need solid walls around me. Even though there's no reason why they should make me feel any safer.

I'm not going outside again. I've got plenty of firewood, and when I run out, I'll chop up the chairs.

The bunkroom smells of urine. I've got a bucket and I've used it a couple of times, and Isaak has lifted his leg against the doorway, although not against my bunk. I don't mind the smell. I like it. It's emphatic and alive.

I'm rereading Gus' book on the natural history of Spitsbergen. I find its stodginess reassuring. Sometimes I break off to talk to Isaak, or read him a bit, and he sweeps the floor with his tail. Sometimes I talk inside my head, and then it's you I'm talking to, Gus.

Strange, that. Even though there's only Isaak to hear, I still can't talk to you out loud, but only in my head. I tell you what's been happening. I rehearse what I'll say if I see you again. That's what keeps me going. The hope that maybe I will see you again.

I can feel my journal strapped to my chest, like a breastplate. Once, I wrote that I felt as if you were my brother, or my best friend. But now I think maybe it's deeper than that. I don't understand, I've never felt like this. And I'm glad I haven't written about it in my journal. I couldn't bear it if you read it and turned away.

And maybe if I do see you again, I'll never find the courage to say anything to your face. So I'm going to be brave and say it now, fearlessly, out loud.

Gus. I love you.

CHAPTER
EIGHTEEN

I wake to darkness and dead cold.

In the instant of waking I know that I'm perceiving what cannot be — and yet it is. I am awake and I see it, it is real. Through the doorway I see it. It is standing in the main room looking out of the north window. It's inside.

Now it's turning towards me. I feel its rage. Its malevolence crushes me to my bunk.

I fumble for my torch. Can't find it. Can't get untangled from the sleeping bag. I knock over the chair beside me. Glass shatters. A stink of paraffin.

I find the torch. The beam veers crazily off scattered shards, a slick of paraffin. Isaak is huddled against my bunk. His eyes bulge as they follow something that moves out of sight behind the doorway.

Panting, I fight my way out of the sleeping bag. The torch slips from my fingers and hits the floor and blinks out. Whimpering, I fall to my knees and grope for it. I can't find it. Can't see my hand in front of my face. I feel for Isaak. He's gone. I try to call him but my throat has closed. Pain shoots through my palms, my knees. I'm crawling on broken glass. My fingers strike wood. Wall or bunk? Where am I?

Footfalls. Heavy. Wet. Uneven. Behind or in front? Which way? Which way?

I feel its rage beating at me. Sucking the air from my lungs.

Isaak is whimpering. I rise to my feet and blunder towards the sound. I crash against something hard, I burn my hands on hot metal and fall. Still that heavy wet irregular tread.

Wheezing, I crawl across the floor. I sense space opening up around me. I see a faint red glimmer. The stove. Christ, I've gone the wrong way. I'm not in the bunkroom. I'm in the main room, there's no way out.

Cornered, I spin round. The stove door is open. I see the glow within. It casts no light, only deepens the blackness. I can't see, but I feel the rage. Close. Coming for me.

Staggering to my feet, I blunder past the stove and into the bunkroom. Darker in here. Hand over hand, I feel my way past the bunks. In my stockinged feet I slip, lurching against the packing cases. The portable stove goes down with a crash. I can't find my way past the packing cases. Can't find the hall. I stumble against something clammy and cold, something that gives beneath my fingers like mouldy sheepskin. Dread clamps my chest. I can't move. My mind is going black. I can't bear it. The rage, the malevolence, I can't . . .

Isaak is scrabbling frantically at the door. I cannon towards the sound. I skin my knuckles on wood. The door. The door. Isaak shoots past me. I'm in the hall. Colder. Darkness presses on my eyeballs. I'm sharply aware of the hatch overhead and the roof space beyond. I feel my way. Guns. Hooks. Waterproofs. Cold stiff sleeves brush my face. My feet tangle in harnesses. Isaak has found the door. I claw at it. I can't find the handle. I'm in the porch, battling a thicket of ski sticks and shovels. I wrench open the door and burst out into the night.

The cold is a wall. I run into it, my feet crunching in snow. Cold rasps my throat, it bites my flesh. No moon. No stars.

194

Only faint grey snowglow to tell up from down. Isaak streaks past me towards the shore. I run after him.

Glancing over my shoulder, I see the cabin windows flickering yellow. They look wrong. That's not the steady glow of lamplight, it's the leap of flames. The cabin is on fire.

I lurch against a boulder. I push myself off and run. I trip over Isaak. He stands tense and still, his ears pricked. Listening.

Clutching his scruff, I hear nothing but the hiss of wind.

Again I glance over my shoulder. The fire in the windows has deepened to orange. Dark against the glare, I glimpse a wet round head. I can't tell if it's inside the cabin or out. It's watching. It knows where I am.

Isaak squirms out of my grip and shoots off. I can't feel my feet, but I stumble after him. My only thought is to get away.

On the shore, the wind numbs my face. The whale ribs glimmer redly. I hear the suck of water, the clink of ice. I've reached the sea. I've nowhere left to go.

I've got no coat, no hat, no boots. I won't last long. I'm past caring. Though I hate the thought of leaving Isaak on his own.

He stands alert, swivelling his ears to catch whatever it is he's hearing. His tail is high. It takes me a moment to understand. He's not afraid any more.

At last I hear what he hears. A distant splash of oars. I blink in disbelief. Now I see it: a point of light rocking on the water. A rowing boat.

A splintering crash behind us as a window blows out. Falling to my knees, I cling to Isaak. The fuel dump by the porch will be next to go.

195

I crouch at the edge of the black water and wait for the boat to pick us up.

Eriksson is at the oars, with Algie and two burly sealers, but it's Gus I see.

Moaning, I splash into the shallows. I fall into his arms.

"Steady, old man, steady. Jack — your *feet*! Where are your boots? Oh, Jack!" His voice is gentle and he's stroking my back and talking all the time, as if I were a dog.

There's a *whump* and a rush of wind, then a deafening boom. We watch blazing debris soar skywards, then crash to earth. The cabin has become a deep red throbbing heart.

Men are lifting me into the boat. I'm moaning for Isaak. Someone throws him on top of me. Now the sealers are pushing off and Gus is wrapping my feet in Algie's muffler and flinging a blanket round my shoulders. Dimly, I make out Algie's white, shocked face. I try to speak but I can't. I can't even shiver.

There's plenty of room in the boat for six men and one dog, but I huddle in the stern, with Gus on one side, Isaak on the other. Isaak is pressed against me. His forelegs are splayed, his claws digging in. He's scared of the sea. Numbly, I see the lights of the *Isbjørn* further out in the bay, blinking her message of sanctuary through the dark. I'm with people. I'm with Gus. I can't take it in.

The boat rocks on the swell as we head for the ship. I lean against Gus and watch Gruhuken burn: a crimson so intense that it hurts to look. I can't drag my gaze away. I stare at the flames shooting into the sky. The fire sends flickering fingers of light towards us over the water. But we're too far out. It can't reach us now.

I begin to shudder. Gus says that's a good sign. He's still talking to me, softly, continuously.

Beside me, Isaak stiffens. I feel his hackles against my cheek. My heart stops. There are seven men in the boat. Next to Gus — a wet round head.

Isaak goes wild. I'm shouting, clutching him, trying to drag Gus away from that thing. Men are yelling, standing up, the boat's rocking wildly. Isaak is desperate to get away, I can't hold him. He's overboard. Gus isn't there any more. I'm screaming his name, reaching for him. I can't get to him, he's too far out.

I jump in after him. The cold is a hammer to my chest. The sea is dragging me down. In the darkness, my hand touches his. I grab it. My chest is bursting. I'm trying to haul him upwards, but my fingers are numb, he slips out of my grip. Flailing, I strike a body. It isn't Gus. My hand clutches something soft as mouldy leather.

I struggle, I kick myself free. Up to the surface, choking, spitting out seawater. I catch a choppy glimpse of the burning camp.

Against the glare, a black figure stands watching on the shore.

CHAPTER
NINETEEN

I didn't die.

The boat didn't capsize, and those on board pulled the survivors from the sea and rushed us back to the ship. For two days I lay in my old bunk, drifting in and out of consciousness.

Algie told me why they'd arrived at Gruhuken when they did. They'd been so concerned after our last wireless exchange that they'd persuaded Eriksson to set off at once. That's what saved me: the fact that I couldn't convince them that nothing was wrong.

It killed Gus. He was the only one who died. One of the sealers fell in too, but was pulled alive from the water, and Mr Eriksson lost the tips of three fingers to frostbite. Algie survived unscathed. Or so he maintains.

Gus' body was never found. Perhaps the current bore him out to sea. Perhaps he never escaped Gruhuken.

I swore I would never write another journal, but yesterday I bought this exercise book. Why? Maybe it's because tomorrow is the tenth anniversary of Gus' death, and I feel the need to give an account of myself. Although I'm not sure to whom.

On the journey to Longyearbyen, we didn't speak of what had happened, but one afternoon, Mr Eriksson visited me in the sickhouse. I wanted to thank him for risking his ship to rescue me; and he wanted (he later wrote) to tell me how sorry he was that he hadn't warned us that Gruhuken is haunted. But who would have believed him? In the end, neither of us could find the words, so we smoked in silence. Then I told him what had happened in the cabin, and what I'd seen in the boat. He kept his eyes on the floor, and when I'd finished, he said, *ja*, the thing in the boat, I saw it also. That's the last time I ever spoke of it.

What I didn't tell him is that Gus saw it too. I glimpsed his face as he went overboard. I can't bear to think of it.

It's my fault that he died. It was for him that I stayed at Gruhuken: because I wanted to impress him. I pitted myself against it, but it was Gus who died. I think of that ten times a day, every day.

A year after we returned to England, I had a letter from Mr Eriksson. He told me he'd gone back to Gruhuken to search for Gus' remains, but hadn't found them. He said he was sorry he hadn't been able to raise a cairn over the bones of our friend. And he said that he'd done what he could to warn others to stay away, by stringing coils of barbed wire along the shore, and "other things" which he didn't describe.

He had no need to explain why he'd done all this. We both know that what we saw that night is still there.

I find it hard to believe that Eriksson had the courage to return to that terrible place. I can't imagine such bravery. I certainly don't have it. But I do seem to possess a rudimentary sense of honour, because I confessed to Gus' parents. I went to see them and told them that when he fell ill, it was my decision to stay at Gruhuken alone. I told them it was because of me that he came back. Because of me that he died.

I thought they'd hate me. But they were *grateful*. Algie had told them how I'd jumped overboard to save their son, and they could see that I was shattered because I'd failed. They thought me the very pattern of what an Englishman should be. They've been wonderful to me, and I can never repay them. They helped us settle things about the insurance and the equipment we'd had on loan, and Gus' father had a "quiet word" which kept the press off the story. They found a specialist for my frostbite, and another to help me adjust after the surgeon amputated my foot. Algie told them about my nightmares and my terror of the dark, and they found a sanatorium — in Oxford, as far from the sea as one can get.

They found this position for me, too. I've been in Jamaica for nine years. I work at the research station of the Botanical Gardens in Castleton. My duties are administrative and botanical. I can no longer tolerate physics. It appals me. And plants bring me closer to Gus.

The work is predictable, and I need that more than anything. I perform each task at a set time, according to the weekly plan I've written in my book. My book also prescribes times for meals, walks, reading, sleeping, gardening and seeing people. Algie says I've become as bad as a German — and he ought to know, after three years as a POW — but I think he understands. I cling to my routine because I lost it once. It reassures me. Even though I know that security is an illusion.

I like Jamaica. The tropical nights are almost the same length all year round, with no lingering twilight to fray the nerves. I like the vivid colours in my garden: the scarlet ginger lilies and yellow cassia trees, the poisonous pink oleanders. I like the incessant, noisy life: the insects and the whistling frogs, the chattering birds.

My house is in the hills, in a jungle of palms and tree ferns, by a towering silk-cotton tree. The locals call it a "duppy tree", "duppy" being the Jamaican word for ghost. That doesn't trouble me. The local idea of ghosts strikes me as touchingly naïve.

My verandah has a view of green mountains. Hummingbirds sip the flowers which hang in curtains from the eaves. There's a stephanotis — my cook says the waxy white blossoms are flowers for the dead — and a climbing vetch she calls "the overlook", as it wards off the evil eye. The road to Castleton is a murmurous tunnel of giant bamboo, and that's good, as it means I can't see the sea. It's only a few miles away, but I never go near it, except once a year.

I still have the journal I wrote at Gruhuken. It was found on me after they hauled me from the sea. As I sit at my desk, I can see it lying on top of my bookcase. It's warped and salt-stained, and I picture my words inside, bleeding together. I've never opened it. I never will.

Gus' shirt was taken off me and destroyed before I regained consciousness, so I have nothing of his. Hugo offered to send me the photograph that was taken of us in Tromsø, dressed up in our new winter gear. I said no. I couldn't bear to see us so hopeful and unaware.

It occurs to me that I haven't mentioned Bjørvik. On our way back to Longyearbyen, Mr Eriksson put in at Wijdefjord and asked the trapper if he wanted to leave with us, but he said no, he would overwinter as planned. He said to tell me he was sorry about my friend, and relieved that I'd survived. Three days before Christmas, two of the dogs, Anadark and Upik, turned up at his camp. They were starving and terrified, but he nursed them back to health, and in the spring he sent word to Algie, asking what should be done. After conferring with me, Algie sent money to compensate for their upkeep, and told Bjørvik to consider them his, with our thanks. He sold them to the mine manager in Longyearbyen for an excellent price. I'm glad. He's a poor man, and the money would have meant a lot to him. And I've no doubt that Upik and Anadark have adapted to life with their new pack.

Of the other dogs — Pakomi, Kiawak, Svarten, Eli and Jens — no trace was ever found.

Isaak is with me. The sealers hauled him out of the sea, and during those first days on the *Isbjørn* he never left my side.

Dogs are a religion to Gus' parents, so they understood that we couldn't be parted. After Isaak had spent months in quarantine, we were reunited, and we've scarcely been separated since.

It's because of Isaak that I took this house, as it catches the sea breeze in the morning and the land breeze in the evening. He's adapted surprisingly well to the heat — by which I mean he's become lazy. I've built him a shady pergola in the garden, with a wading pool, which he loves. We take our walks in the cool of the dawn, and although there are no rabbits, he's the terror of the mongoose community. Twice a day, we have the ceremony of de-ticking. He adores that, as it means he has all my attention. He more than holds his own with the local mastiffs, and some of the puppies born to the neighbourhood bitches have a distinctly husky-ish appearance.

I don't know what I would have done without him. He's my best friend, the only living creature I can really talk to, and a precious link with Gus.

In his undemonstrative way, Algie has also become a good friend, although in the beginning I blamed him; he should never have allowed Gus to come on the rescue mission. Then I realised that Algie blames himself quite enough already, without me making it worse.

I value his friendship, but we never talk of Gruhuken. He's never spoken of his experiences there, nor asked about mine. So that is always between us.

Occasionally, I correspond with Hugo, but I've only seen him once. It wasn't a success. We both knew that he is on one side of the divide, and I on the other. Because he never saw Gruhuken.

My life here is a good one, I think. It's only in October and November that I have a bad time. When I wake to darkness and I'm back in the polar night, hearing a heavy wet irregular tread.

Every year on the anniversary of Gus' death, I make my pilgrimage to an isolated beach on the north coast, where I can be sure of being alone. I go at midday, when the sun is at its fiercest, but I still have to nerve myself to do it. I don't sleep well for a week before. But I haven't funked it yet.

The sea here is nothing like Gruhuken. Tiny fishes dart in the turquoise water, and pelicans glide overhead. But it's the same sea. And though I stand on this white sand before the warm little waves, I know that at Gruhuken, it's the deep of the polar night.

When I've mustered my courage, I can just bring myself to crouch at the water's edge and dip in my hand, and hold it there while I talk to Gus. It's a kind of communion. But it's a dangerous one, for I know that I'm also communing with Gruhuken, and with what walks there in the dark.

When I sat down to write this, I didn't know who it was for, but I do now. This is for you, Gus. This is how things have been since I lost you.

And maybe tomorrow when I go down to the sea, I'll burn these pages and scatter the ashes on the waves, and they'll reach you, wherever you are.

Recently, I've begun to wonder if perhaps your parents were right not to blame me for your death. Perhaps you didn't come back to Gruhuken to save me, but only to salvage the expedition. Maybe you didn't feel for me what I felt — what I still feel — for you. I'll never know.

But I can take that. It's not the worst of it. The worst is not knowing if you're still there. Are you, Gus? Are you there in the black water? Do you walk on the shore, in the dead grey stillness among the bones? Or were you snuffed out like a spark, all trace extinguished? Oh, I hope so. I can't bear to think of you still there.

Because I know that I can never go back. Not even for you, Gus. Not even when I remember how it was in the beginning: the guillemots on the cliffs and the seals slipping through the green water, and the ice talking to itself in the bay.

THE END

Author's Note

I first visited Spitsbergen in summer 2007, when I travelled by ship around the whole archipelago, putting in at many beautiful, desolate places, including ruined mines and trappers' camps. I've drawn on that voyage for Jack's experiences at the time of the midnight sun, and for his initial impressions of Gruhuken. Last winter I returned to Spitsbergen — to reacquaint myself with huskies, to do some snowshoeing in the dark, and to get the feel of the polar night.

Concerning Spitsbergen as it was in the early twentieth century, including the lives of trappers, sealers, and those who made scientific expeditions to the islands, I'm particularly indebted to the following: *The Diaries of Thorleif Bjertnes (Nordaustlandet 1933–34)* (translated by Lee Carmody, Svalbard Museum, 2000); *Spitsbergen: An Account of the Exploration, Hunting, Mineral Riches and Future Potentialities of an Arctic Archipelago* (R. N. R. Brown, London, 1920); *A woman in the Polar Night* (C. Ritter, London, 1955); *With Seaplane and Sledge in the Arctic* (G. Binney, New York, 1926); *Under the Pole Star — The Oxford University Arctic Expedition 1935–6* (A. R. Glen, London, 1937).

★ ★ ★

However I should make it clear that the characters in the story are imaginary, and weren't intended to resemble any of those who took part in the real expeditions, which for the most part had happier outcomes than Jack's. And in case anyone is tempted to seek Gruhuken on the map, it doesn't exist. Moreover it's not to be confused with the headland named Gråhuken, where a redoubtable trapper's wife once overwintered (see *A Woman in the Polar Night*, above). I made Gruhuken up, and as far as I know, its precise topography isn't to be found in Spitsbergen.

I'd like to thank the people of Longyearbyen for their warmth and helpfulness, especially my guides on numerous occasions, as well as the friendly and diligent staff of the fascinating Svalbard Museum. As always, my thanks go to my publishers, Orion, for their boundless enthusiasm and support, particularly my editor Jon Wood and assistant editor Jade Chandler; and to my wonderful agent, Peter Cox, who has encouraged me since I first mooted the idea for this story, almost a decade ago.

Finally, I'd like to stress that although Jack's impressions of Longyearbyen in 1937 were dismal, it has changed a bit since then. I've always found it a delightful place, both in summer and winter. It's well worth a visit, whether you love the Arctic or are simply curious to experience life in the far north.

Michelle Paver, 2010

Also available in ISIS Large Print:

In the Dead of Night

Alex Crowe

You can't go home again . . .

Lost in the mist in the Lake District, the lives of six strangers become entwined when they seek shelter in the deserted old house. All are running from different things — Amanda from a murder charge; City Boy Mark from financial ruin; Jilly from something she dares not confront; Angus and Dawn from his wife.

The house has been recently occupied. The lights are on, a fire still burns, there's a half-eaten meal on the table. But then they discover that the phone is dead and the TV cable has been sliced through. Something far worse awaits them here from which they can never escape . . .

ISBN 978-0-7531-8780-7 (hb)
ISBN 978-0-7531-8781-4 (pb)

The Haunting of Gad's Hall

Norah Lofts

No one dared reveal the truth about the haunting of Gad's hall.

No one at Gad's Hall could admit what they knew about the room in the attic. The locked room that held the Thorley family's most shameful secret. The terrifying room that had once been the living tomb of a beautiful young woman possessed by the darkest evil. Years had passed but the relentless diabolic force abided — waiting until it could once again possess an innocent and inflict its horror upon the living. It was a force countless centuries old. It was simply a matter of time before it would strike again. And when the Spender family moved into Gad's Hall, that time had come . . .

ISBN 978-0-7531-8558-2 (hb)
ISBN 978-0-7531-8559-9 (pb)

The Gate of Air

James Buchan

The Gate of Air is written tremendously well . . . deeply thoughtful **Telegraph**

Nothing short of magical **Guardian**

Hauntingly convincing **Independent**

Jim Smith, ousted from his computer software company, retreats to lick his wounds in an old house in a remote farming county in the West of England. Though he knows nothing of country life, he takes on livestock and crops, a dog and a labourer named John Walker of mysterious and independent habits. One night Jim dreams of a beautiful woman. The dream figure seems to correspond with a portrait on the wall of a neighbour's house, of a famous model of the 1960's, Jean Lampard, who vanished in 1967.

At dinner with the local magnate and his wife, Jim sees a ghost. All the certainties and reassurances of modern life vanish, and Jim must deal alone with forces as old as his fields and woods.

ISBN 978-0-7531-8388-5 (hb)
ISBN 978-0-7531-8389-2 (pb)

The Serpent's Tooth

Michelle Paver

A richly satisfying novel of love, friendship and a world changed forever . . .

Since she was twelve years old, Belle has lived with a secret — a secret that cuts her off from her family and isolates her wherever she goes. Against the unfolding horror of the Great War, her search for peace takes her from the brittle gaiety of English country house society to the remote Scottish mansions where her grandmother's tragedy was played out, and to the battlefields of Flanders. As the scarred and shattered men return from the trenches, and the influenza epidemic scythes across the country, Belle must finally discover a way to break free of her secret — or lose her last chance of happiness.

ISBN 978-0-7531-6819-6 (hb)
ISBN 978-0-7531-6820-2 (pb)